A BRUSH WITH MURDER

PAINT AND SIP COZY MYSTERIES, BOOK 1

DONNA CLANCY

SUMMER PRESCOTT BOOKS PUBLISHING

Copyright 2024 Summer Prescott Books

All Rights Reserved. No part of this publication nor any of the information herein may be quoted from, nor reproduced, in any form, including but not limited to: printing, scanning, photocopying, or any other printed, digital, or audio formats, without prior express written consent of the copyright holder.

**This book is a work of fiction. Any similarities to persons, living or dead, places of business, or situations past or present, is completely unintentional.

To my family and friends who believe in me even when I don't believe in myself.

ONE

"We are good for another year," Jannelle said, waving a piece of paper in the air as she came through the front door.

"I can't believe we have been in business for a whole year," Anita replied.

"This new liquor permit says we have been," Jannelle said, tacking it to the wall above the register over the previous year's permit. "And business is booming, even in the off season."

"I know. Here it is October, and we have a full class for tonight; sixteen students in all. Although I think some of them are here for the wine and socializing more so than the painting."

"Does it really matter? As long as they keep coming back," Jannelle said.

Jannelle Brewster, a sixty-five-year-old retired art teacher and her best friend, Anita Prowle, decided to open the Paint and Sip after a night of drinking wine and painting together. They had so much fun they wanted to offer the same kind of enjoyment to other people. Anita's husband, Sid, thought they were crazy but said he would back them if they went into business for themselves.

"What kind of wine are we offering tonight?" Anita asked.

"The new wine shipment should be delivered shortly. What do you say we take a bottle out when it gets here and test it?" Jannelle asked. "Just to make sure it's okay for our customers to drink. We wouldn't want them to drink something not up to our standards, now, would we?"

"You and your wine. It's a wonder we show any profit at all with what you drink in the name of taste testing," Anita said, laughing.

"We want to keep our customers happy," Jannelle said, grabbing a bottle of peach wine from under the counter. "On second thought, this is from the last shipment, and we haven't tried it yet."

"If we are going to serve this tonight, we need to put at least twelve bottles in the fridge to get them nice and cool for the tasting."

"Way ahead of you. I put a case in the fridge out back this morning when I first got here," Jannelle said. "I'm going to go take out a cool one and put this one in its place," Jannelle said, heading for the back room. "I think the new apple wine coming in would be appropriate for the second choice seeing as it is apple picking season."

"Apple wine with a hint of cinnamon. I don't pick out many of the wines we serve but that one caught my fancy," Anita stated.

"You love apple anything," Jannelle said, turning the corkscrew into the top of the bottle of peach wine.

The cork came out with a loud pop. Jannelle waved the bottle back and forth under her nose sniffing the wine at each pass and then inhaling deeply.

"Peachy, really peachy. Pass the glasses, please," she requested. "I can't wait to try this."

Jannelle poured two glasses of the wine and handed one to her friend. She swished it around in the glass and took a sip.

"Can you say yum? I'll be getting a case of this for my personal stock at home," Jannelle said, taking a larger drink from her glass. "What do you think?"

"I think it's one of the sweetest wines I've ever tasted," Anita said, taking a second drink. "It's good. I have a feeling we'll be re-ordering this for the summer classes."

"Now, we have to set up the classroom for the class. Did you bring up the eleven by fourteen canvases from the cellar while I was gone?"

"I did and I set up the mountain landscape painting they'll be copying tonight at the front of the class on the easel. I love the colors of the trees in that painting, and I can't wait to see what color schemes the students use in their paintings."

"I did that painting many years ago while I was at a retreat up in Vermont and it is still one of the favorite paintings the students like to copy," Jannelle stated.

"Who doesn't love autumn colors? Sid and I still take a day trip to New Hampshire every September to view the foliage. And, on the way back we stop at our favorite apple picking farm and load up on everything apple."

"You and Sid have such a great life together. You like so many of the same things and have so much in common. Sometimes I am envious of what you have with your husband."

"I am pretty lucky. I got one of the good ones," Anita said.

Anita and Sid Prowle had been married for forty-one years. They married young and raised their family of two daughters and one son. They were now empty nesters and had four grandchildren with another one on the way. Sid was a postman for Denniston and had the same mail delivery route for over thirty years. He could retire any time he wanted to, but he claimed being a mailman and walking his route six days a week kept him in shape and young at heart.

Jannelle, on the other hand, had married in her mid-thirties to a local trucker. She never wanted children and spent her time teaching art at the local high school. The night of their ten-year anniversary party, Jannelle found out her husband had not only been logging miles but lengthening his list of affairs while out on the road.

One of his flings was a local woman who had the nerve to show her face at the party and after having one too many drinks began bragging about how she went out on the road with Jannelle's husband. Jannelle and her close friends left the party. The next day she hired an attorney and filed for divorce. She buried herself in her art to get over the hurt and never looked back. Meeting another man was not listed in her top ten priorities of life.

"Have you seen Picasso lately?" Jannelle asked, rolling out a clean plastic covering over the tables.

"The last I saw him he was curled up in a ball in the front window enjoying the sunshine. I think he's still there."

Picasso was a male calico cat who Jannelle had rescued from a box left in front of the local library. He was, to the best of Jannelle's estimate, about ten to twelve weeks old when he was abandoned. Every night she took him home and every day while the shop was open he came to visit with the customers.

One day, quite by accident, Picasso stepped on the easel Jannelle was using to paint a new winter picture to use for class. When she turned around, she saw the cat had tracked paw prints down the plastic covering of the table. An idea hit her out of the blue. She called him back to her and had him walk around the same area a few more times.

She waited for the paint to dry and then stretched the plastic onto a wooden frame. The picture was set in the front window with Picasso's name written in the bottom corner of the painting. A sign explaining it was the resident cat's artwork and if sold the money would go to the local rescue in Picasso's name.

The picture was only in the window two short hours before it was snapped up by the local librarian, Fran Dower, to display in the library lobby. The cat's artistic talent made the front page of the newspaper and since that day, Picasso had created and sold more than a dozen pawprint paintings and the Denniston Rescue had been the recipient of all the receipts.

Jannelle made it perfectly clear to people wanting to buy the cat's artwork they didn't force the cat to create the pieces. They only happened by accident which made the pieces more desirable and helped them sell faster. Picasso had become a hometown celebrity helping his fellow shelter animals.

Anita placed easels at each seat and cans with various sized brushes down the center of each table. Most return customers brought their own brushes to use but some of the newer customers came with nothing of their own and needed the supplies offered to them. A metal table-top easel with an eleven by fourteen canvas was set in front of each stool.

Tubes of acrylic paints were placed on the head table where the students could go to load their palettes with the colors they wanted to use for their creations. On a small side table, plastic wine glasses were stacked around the two ice buckets which would keep the wine chilled while the students painted.

"I'm glad we posted the new rule near the door. Some people can hold their wine better than others and I don't want any trouble with the police even though the police chief's wife is here all the time," Anita said, looking over the newly added sign.

It stated that all keys of anyone driving would be turned in upon arrival to either Jannelle or Anita. If a person was too tipsy at the end of the night's class a taxi would be called to take them home and they could return the following day to retrieve their car. It protected the Paint and Sip from lawsuits and their students from unfortunate accidents on the road. If the person did not agree to turn their keys over they were sent home.

"We have to be so careful now-a-days," Jannelle replied. "Well, look who decided to make his presence known."

Picasso had jumped down from the front display window and stopped to stretch. He meowed as if acknowledging the two women and headed to the backroom where his litter box and food were kept.

After his nap in the warm morning sun, it was time to explore and play. He had more toys in the backroom than the local pet store had in stock to sell. The customers constantly brought him new gifts and after he played with the catnip mice he would tear around the shop on a catnip high getting into mischief. That was when he did his best painting.

Every couple of months, Jannelle would go through the toys and take the unused and new ones to the shelter for the cats there to play with and enjoy. Picasso had his favorites and never missed the toys when they disappeared. The two women never told the customers the extra toys went to the shelter because they were afraid the influx of toys for Picasso would stop and the shelter cats would lose out.

"It's almost time for a new creation from Picasso," Anita stated. "I hear they are running short on certain types of food and supplies at the shelter, and they could use the donation."

"I guess I have time to paint a new winter landscape for our students to copy in the November classes. We'll see if Picasso feels like being creative today," Jannelle said, laughing.

The next two hours, Jannelle sat at the table in the backroom painting. Anita retired to the office to catch up on the books and pay some bills. Picasso had been playing with the catnip for quite a while and was running around the shop. Jannelle set some plastic on the floor next to where she was sitting with some small smudges of paint in the corners on the chance the cat would run through it.

An hour later, Jannelle was done with the painting and the cat hadn't gone near the plastic. As a matter of fact, the cat hadn't been in the backroom in quite a while. She went looking for him and found him back in the front window, stretched out in the sun, sleeping soundly.

"I see how it is. Ye ole catnip wins again," Jannelle said, smiling at the shop mascot. "I guess we'll have to make our own donation to the shelter so they can get the food they need for your friends there."

"I'm going home to cook an early supper for Sid. Do you want me to bring you back some meatloaf and mashed potatoes?" Anita asked, coming out of the office.

"No, thank you, I'm good. I made a lasagna on my day off and I'm still eating the leftovers," her friend answered.

"Okay, I'll be back before six. Are you going to stay here to accept the wine order? Devon is really late today," Anita asked.

"I'll be here. We won't have time to chill the apple wine, so we'll have to offer the pink Zin already chilling in the fridge."

"I left the checks on the desk for your signature. We actually did good this month and are in the black in the wine account. Things will get busier and more profitable with the holidays approaching."

"I'm sure they will. We did really well last year at Christmas and the business has grown in repeat customers since then."

"See you in a while," Anita said, closing the front door.

Picasso lifted his head at the sound of the door, but seeing no one new in the area, he closed his eyes and went back to sleep.

"You have got to be one of the laziest cats I have ever seen," his owner stated, smiling. "Eat and sleep. The life of a cat."

The checks were sitting on the desk for her to sign. When they opened the accounts it was decided they would require both of their signatures on any checks written for the business. That way, they were both involved in the running of the business, and both would know the status of the balances in the various accounts.

She signed the checks and tacked them to the cork board above the desk. They would be mailed the following morning. Jannelle knew they could do all this online, but she didn't feel like she had control of things doing it that way. Anita and she agreed the old-fashioned way was the best for them, hand-written checks, and ledgers.

They did all their ordering online which was a huge step for them in trying to exist in the modern world of technology. Before they opened the Paint and Sip, both women had only dabbled in social media and done nothing else on their computers.

Sid stepped up and taught them how to order their supplies by computer and not by phone. Once they got the swing of things they liked the convenience of ordering online, but they couldn't bring themselves to do banking online.

Jannelle gathered together the supplies she needed to complete the new project for Saturday afternoon's class. Not only did they offer painting at night, but they also offered craft classes. This week they would be making winter wreaths out of vines, glitter pinecones, and a variety of greens and holly. And if the student liked the look, they could finish the wreath by spraying it with fake snow.

She fashioned the vines into a circle and fastened them together with wire. Jannelle set the wreath down on the table and turned her attention to what she wanted to decorate it with so she could hang it on the front door of the shop for all to see as they passed by and maybe stir up some additional interest in the weekend class.

Forgetting the green tartan ribbon to make the bow for the wreath, she went to storage to get the spool of ribbon. When she returned to the classroom area, she couldn't help but laugh. Picasso had left the window and was sitting in the center of the wreath while batting around the pinecones on the table.

"Sure, you can get into my crafting things, but you couldn't paint me a picture earlier," Jannelle said to the cat as she moved him to the floor.

The cat wandered off not looking back. Jannelle could hear the crunching sound of the cat snacking on his dry food. She finished her wreath and held it up to look at to make sure things were straight and spaced properly. Silver glitter pinecones were spaced out evenly between sprigs of holly and red berries. The Scottish tartan ribbon was made into a full bow and wired onto the bottom center of the wreath.

"I may have to make another one of these for my own door at home," she said, walking to the front door to hang it for all to see.

She checked her watch, and it was almost five o'clock.

I wonder where Devon is with our wine delivery. He's usually here no later than two o'clock.

At five forty-five, Anita returned from her trip home. She brought a container with her which held homemade apple crisp and a side tub of whipped cream. She set it in the fridge out back for Jannelle to eat later.

The ice buckets were filled with ice cubes and one bottle of each kind of wine. A cheese tray and fruit tray were set on the same table along with small dessert plates. The first customers started to arrive shortly after six. The actual lesson did not begin until six-thirty, which gave everyone a half an hour to socialize and get their wine before selecting a seat where they would paint. Tonight's students were a lot of the older locals in town. Everyone knew everyone and the buzz was quite loud as the time approached to start painting.

"Let's pick our seats, shall we?" Jannelle announced. "You've all had a chance to look at tonight's painting close up so it shouldn't be an issue where you sit."

The women grabbed their wine glasses and chose a seat. Jannelle started to walk them through the laying out of the picture. She had a large pad of paper on an easel and drew each step the women needed to do to block in on the canvas. When the first step was complete the students proceeded to the table at the head of the room to fill their palettes with the colors they chose to use.

Anita's job was to keep the wine bottles full and on ice. She walked around periodically refilling the women's glasses if they wanted their drinks topped off. She herself was an accomplished artist but chose to stay in the background while Jannelle taught the classes. A couple of times, here and there, she would teach a class but preferred to socialize instead of instructing.

Once the students had their colors and started painting, both Jannelle and Anita walked around to answer questions or help with any issues that arose. Around seven o'clock, a loud bang was heard coming from the backroom. Anita went to investigate.

The back door was open, and a cardboard box was visible. Anita went to stand guard at the door so Picasso couldn't get out into the darkness as she knew the wine delivery was finally arriving, five hours late. She opened the door for Devon as he had a full hand truck of boxes full of wine.

"Fourteen more in the truck," he said, smiling. "Do you want them down cellar?"

"Please. Why are you so late today?" Anita asked.

"Stupid truck broke down again. She's getting old and can't take this cooler weather so well anymore. It will probably get worse as winter sets in."

Devon Banister was in his mid-thirties and quite handsome. Sandy blond hair and bright blue eyes, to look at him you would think he was straight out of a beach movie set in California. His muscles were huge and well defined as he had been delivering cases of wine and beer since he was in his early twenties.

His reputation as a player was well known around town. He was pleasant to everyone, especially to the local women. Jannelle liked him but always said it must be something about truck driving that turned men into Casanovas. He made five more trips to the truck and back leaving the cases of apple wine upstairs as Anita requested.

"Would you like a cup of coffee?" Anita asked. "I think there is a few donuts left, too."

"That's sounds great. I haven't eaten since this morning," Devon answered, taking off his work gloves.

They walked out into the main classroom and all the women looked up to see who had caused the commotion out in the back room. Many of them recognized Devon and broad smiles broke out on their faces. The older women smoothed their hair, and the younger women batted their eyes and smiled at him.

"Hello, everyone," Devon said, picking up a coffee cup.

A few of them left their seats and gravitated toward the handsome delivery man. Millie Stanton, the police chief's wife, made her way to where Jannelle and Anita were standing.

"All four of those women are seeing Devon on the side," she whispered.

"Seriously? Even Kristin Desmond, the selectman's wife?" Anita whispered back.

"Yes, even her. He is a very busy delivery man, and his harem gets larger with each passing week. All the women compete for his time and attention. It's pretty funny to watch actually."

"Devon, I'm having trouble with my garbage disposal," Sally Andrews, the owner of the local hair salon said. "Do you think you could come take a look at it for me?"

"Sure, not a problem," he replied, smiling.

"You promised to look at the cable hook-up in my house this weekend. Something is not right with it and the cable keeps cutting out," Kristen said.

"Why don't you call the cable company to fix it?" Sally asked nastily.

"Here we go," Millie said, smiling.

"Because it costs too much money for them to come to the house. Not that it's any of your business anyway," Kristen replied, throwing daggers Sally's way. "Why don't you call a plumber?"

"Ladies, ladies. I can get to you all, don't worry," Devon said, loving the attention and the fact the women were fighting over him.

"He sure will, and we all know Kristen's husband will be gone all weekend for a conference in Boston," Millie said to Jannelle and Anita.

"I need to pay more attention to the gossip around here. I had no idea any of this was going on in our little town. I mean, I knew Devon was seeing several women at the same time but not married women," Jannelle said.

"Let's see. There's Polly and Aria from the salon, Sherry, Larry the electrician's wife, and probably many more in other towns we don't know about," Matilda, the fire chief's wife said, joining the group.

"My, our delivery man keeps himself busy," Anita stated.

"I wonder how many husbands know what's going on?" Jannelle replied.

"I don't know but I'm sure the damn is going to break eventually, and someone's husband will do something about Romeo," Millie said.

"Ladies, let's get back to our paintings, please," Jannelle announced.

"See you this weekend," Sally said to Devon.

"In your dreams," Kristen said, walking by them.

Devon grabbed a couple of donuts, refilled his coffee cup, and left.

The rest of the evening, the four women who showed an interest in the delivery man glared at each other from behind their easels. The other women in the room were amused at what was taking place. One by one the paintings were finished and the artist holding their completed project had their picture taken for the wall. Shortly after ten, the last customer left.

"Well, that was one interesting evening," Anita said, pulling the used top layer off one of the disposable easels.

"It sure was. You learn something new at each one of these classes," Jannelle replied. "Put lots of women together in one room and you never know what will happen."

"Do you think what Matilda said will come true? Do you think someone's husband will find out and something will happen to Devon?"

"I don't think so, not in our little town. They may teach him a lesson and issue a threat, but I don't think anything worse than that will happen," Jannelle replied, collecting the cans of paintbrushes off the tables. "I'm tired. What say we head home and finish cleaning up in the morning?"

"Sounds good to me. I think Picasso is under the table in the back room," Anita replied.

Jannelle put Picasso's cat carrier on the floor in front of him. He was so used to going back and forth from the house to the shop and back again, he offered no resistance and walked into the carrier by himself.

The front door was locked, the lights turned off, and the two women left by the back door alarming the shop on the way out.

TWO

The sun was shining brightly on Friday morning when Jannelle crawled out of bed. Picasso had been awake for a few hours and was somewhere in the house getting into mischief. She took her coffee and stepped out on to the screened-in porch at the front of her house. The October air was brisk, and Jannelle inhaled deeply taking the coolness into her lungs.

Picasso strolled out onto the porch. He jumped up on the back of the couch and sat watching the bird feeder, his tail swishing back and forth. His head followed the birds as they flew by going to and from the feeder. When a bird flew a little too close to the window, he would bat at the screen attempting to take the bird down in flight.

"Good thing there is a screen between you and my feathery friends," she said to the cat, scratching behind his ear. "Do you want some breakfast?"

Picasso knew that word and jumped down off the couch and headed for the kitchen. His owner set down a plate of his favorite wet food and went to refill her coffee. She returned to the porch and sat in the rocking chair closest to the feeders.

Opening the shop at ten o'clock had been Anita's idea. She wanted the mornings off to get her various errands done and to be able to have breakfast with her husband before he left for his mail route. Jannelle had protested opening so late at first, but the more mornings she spent on her porch with her coffee and the birds the more she grew to like the idea.

After all, she was semi-retired and deserved a little time for herself. It was quite the opposite of when she had to be at school every morning by seven to start teaching her first class at seven-thirty. And Jannelle still had two days off from the shop, Sunday and Monday, which was equivalent to her weekends off when she was an art teacher.

Jannelle finished her second cup of coffee, shooed the cat inside, then closed and locked the front door so she could go upstairs and take a shower. She had to go to the Denniston Shelter before she went to work to drop off the check for them to buy some of the food they needed for the animals.

Picasso followed her into the bathroom and batted at her shadow on the shower curtain as she showered. On more than one occasion the cat had slipped off the edge of the tub and landed in the water at Jannelle's feet. Hating the feeling of getting wet, the cat would attempt to quickly jump out of the tub getting tangled in the curtain on the way out. Jannelle always found him drying himself off on the shelf below the bay window.

"Enjoy the sunshine in the window," Jannelle said, picking up her purse. "You can stay home and have the house to yourself. I'll be home early as there are no classes today. I filled your dry food and water dispenser so you should be fine. I'll see you in a few hours."

The cat didn't even acknowledge the fact that his owner was speaking to him and continued preening himself in the warm sunshine.

"Independent little cuss," Jannelle mumbled as she closed the front door.

The parking lot at The Denniston Rescue League was full. Jannelle hoped the reason was that people were coming to adopt the animals, but deep down she knew most of the cars were there to see Mary Kramer, the vet, whose office was located in the back of the rescue building.

She sat in her car, watching a family she recognized from school functions proudly coming out of the front door with an older dog leading the way. The dad held a big bag of food, and the mom had some toys and treats in her hands. Tommy was smiling from ear to ear as he opened the car door for the dog to jump into the back seat. He couldn't quite get in, so the dad helped the dog, picking him up and placing him in the seat next to Tommy.

One furever home. That makes me so happy. Seniors need love, too.

Jannelle used to foster animals for Dr, Kramer but since opening the Paint and Sip she found she had less time to take care of the younger ones that needed around the clock attention. Occasionally she would still take in an older dog who was having trouble dealing with the noise and confusion at the shelter and needed quiet around them. She would end up keeping them until they crossed over the Rainbow Bridge, making sure their final years had been golden ones and they had received all the love they deserved.

"Long time no see," Cindy Pummel said as Jannelle came through the door. "I was going to call you today."

"It has been a while, hasn't it? What's up?"

"Are you up for the idea of another senior to foster?"

"Why? Do you have one who needs out of here?" Jannelle asked.

"We do. Mrs. Sanderson passed away last week, and she had no family to take her fourteen-year-old dog, Petunia. She is tiny, only six pounds and sits in the corner of the cage petrified at every sound made around her."

"Is that the little dachshund I used to see her walking around Main Street?"

"It is. She is the sweetest little baby. Do you think you could foster her?" Cindy asked. "She is used to a quiet house with Mrs. Sanderson and not the hubbub of the kennels here."

"Has she ever been around cats before?"

"Mrs. Sanderson had two cats at one time so I'm sure Petunia remembers them. Besides, Picasso has never had a problem with any of the other fosters you have taken in."

"I know. It's just with the shop to run now, it makes it kind of hard to have a dog around that needs to go out. I suppose I could bring Petunia to the shop with me and put a gate up to keep her in the back room."

"She's pretty chill. Most of the time she sleeps because of her age. Think about it. She's a wreck here and the sooner she gets out of here the better," Cindy said. "Now, what can I help you with today?"

"I came by to drop off this check from Picasso. We heard you needed food for the animals, and he wanted to help," Jannelle said, placing the check on the counter in front of Cindy.

"Did he sell another painting?" Cindy asked.

"No, not this time. He just wanted to help his friends here."

"This will buy quite a bit of food. Tell Picasso thank you very much," Cindy said, coming out from behind the counter and giving Jannelle a big hug. "You are a special person, you know that?"

"Wasn't me, it was the cat. I'll be back in a few hours to get Petunia. I have to get some supplies for at home and a gate and dog bed for the shop before I can take her. Do you have a carrier big enough for her so I can take her home?"

"We have some which have been donated from other customers. I'm sure we have one you can take for her."

"I guess I have time to go meet with Petunia. Can you take me to her?" Jannelle asked.

"Sure, follow me."

In the back corner of the kennels, as isolated as good as she could be, sat Petunia in her little cage. She picked her head up and looked at Jannelle and then laid down facing the corner of the cage.

"I told you she's not doing so well," Cindy stated.

"That will change as of today," Jannelle said, opening the door and sitting on the floor in front of the opening. "Petunia, come here girl."

The dog turned her head and stared at the person who called her by name.

"Come see me. It's okay, you'll be okay. You're going home with me today. Would you like that?"

Petunia stood up and slowly walked to the door of the cage. She sniffed Jannelle's extended hand and nudged it to be patted. Cautiously, she climbed into Jannelle's crossed legs and let out a big sigh.

"She trusts you," Cindy said, happy the meeting was going so well.

"I think she might remember me. Mrs. Sanderson used to walk by the shop, and I would bring a treat out for Petunia," she replied, gently stroking the dog's head. "You have found a new home, Miss Petunia. I know you miss your mama, but we'll try hard to make sure you feel loved again."

"I believe Mrs. Sanderson is smiling down and extremely happy Petunia is going to a new home with you," Cindy said. "I'll fill out the paperwork and have everything ready to go when you come back later. I knew you wouldn't let Petunia down."

"NO, you know I am a softie," Jannelle said, smiling. "I'll be back to get you."

Jannelle sat in her car making a list of all the items she needed to pick up before returning to get Petunia. She would check in at the shop and because there were no classes scheduled for today, she would be free to leave to complete her shopping and pick up the dog.

Anita was already at the shop and waiting on a couple customers who had come in for art supplies. Jannelle told her friend about the dog and how she needed to go shopping and get the dog out of the noisy kennel today. Anita said she would be more than happy to watch the shop as she remembered the dog and was sorry Mrs. Sanderson had passed.

"I am going to buy a gate to keep her in the back room but if it's too noisy for her, I might put a bed in the office where we can close the door and it would be quiet," Jannelle stated.

"Is Picasso going to be all right with a new roommate?"

"You know him. It's like he knows they need a place to go, and it doesn't bother him when another animal comes into the house."

"He is kind of special that way," Anita replied. "If you want, take the day off and get Petunia and Picasso to know each other at home before you bring them both here," Anita suggested.

"You don't mind? I think the only thing going on today is the wine delivery and that's only fourteen cases. You can have Devon put it all right downstairs."

"You will be here for tomorrow's wreath making class, right?"

"I will. Thanks for covering for me. And Petunia thanks you."

"Anything for the animals, you know that," Anita said, smiling. "Go! Get that baby out of all the noise and make her feel safe and loved again."

She completed her shopping and returned to the shelter. Cindy had found a crate which was just the right size for Petunia, and it was sitting outside the cage. When Jannelle approached the dog it was almost like she recognized her and came right up to the wire door, tail wagging.

Cindy opened the door and Petunia went right to Jannelle who picked her up and talked softly to her, asking her if she was ready to go to her new home. The dog gave her new owner a kiss and laid her head on Jannelle's shoulder,

"It's like she knows you came to rescue her," Cindy said, tearing up.

"They know," Jannelle replied. "And I have a funny feeling Petunia is no longer a foster but adopted, she's found her permanent new home. Now, in the carrier you go so we can get out of here."

She put the dog on the floor who walked into the carrier all by herself with no nudging from anyone. Petunia turned a couple of circles and nestled down in the blanket, ready to go.

"You two are made for each other," Cindy said.

"You say that every time I leave here with a new foster," Jannelle replied.

"Yes, I do. But I know they will never come back here again, and they will have a long life, loved and cared for by you right until the end."

"I'm sure the customers will love on her, too," Jannelle said, picking up the carrier. "Now the shop will have two mascots."

"I'll check in with you in a few days to see how things are going," Cindy said, opening the front door for the pair to leave. "Give Picasso a hug for me."

She arrived home to find the cat still perched in the bay window. He opened his eyes and spotted the carrier that Jannelle set down on the floor near where he was laying. Picasso jumped down out of the window and sauntered up to the front of the carrier. He sniffed at the door where Petunia was standing looking out. Not bothered at all by the new resident, the cat walked into the kitchen.

"Step two; let's see how it goes with Petunia out of the carrier," Jannelle said, opening the door.

The dog exited the carrier all the while looking around for the cat. She sniffed the furniture, tail wagging, and kept turning around looking for Jannelle to make sure she hadn't gone too far away from her. Picasso returned from the kitchen, and they ended up nose to nose. Not the least bit impressed with the dog, the cat jumped back up into the window and lay there watching every movement Petunia made.

The dog wandered into the kitchen and found the cat's food. She tested some of the dry food, didn't seem to like it and then took a long drink of water from the dispenser.

"Don't like the cat food, huh?" Jannelle mumbled. "We need to find you your own space for your food dish. Let's see."

She walked around the kitchen with the dog in tow looking for a good spot to put her food. She settled on the corner of the kitchen next to the pantry door and turned to say something to the dog, but she wasn't there. A faint whining could be heard coming from the mudroom off the kitchen.

Petunia was standing at the door scratching at the bottom of it to go out. She turned to look at her new owner and scratched some more.

"What a smart girl," Jannelle said to the dog as she went to get her leash.

Picasso watched out the bay window as Jannelle and Petunia walked the perimeter of the yard. The dog sniffed every inch before finding a suitable place to do her business. Back inside the dog took a drink of water and found her bed in the living room. She sighed a deep sigh and closed her eyes.

"Poor thing. Probably hasn't had a moments peace since arriving at the rescue," Jannelle said, talking to Picasso who had come to the edge of the shelf to see where the dog went. "It's nice and quiet. She should sleep for a while. You have been a good cat accepting your new roommate, so far anyway."

Jannelle made some lunch for herself and sat in her favorite recliner to eat. She turned on one of her soaps that she no longer had time to watch because of opening the shop. She soon discovered while not watching the soap for almost a year, not much had changed in the storyline. A few new characters had joined the cast but other than that nothing had changed.

"Well, that was a waste of time. I'll never understand what I saw in them in the first place," she said to Picasso who had jumped up in her lap looking for something to eat.

She gave the cat some turkey and ate the last bite herself. Petunia had slept through the meal, not waking up once. Seeing there was nothing else for him to eat, Picasso disappeared into the kitchen where his owner could hear him taking a drink.

Jannelle had just closed her eyes to take a quick nap while the dog did, when her cell phone rang. She had left it in her purse and had to run to the kitchen to answer it.

"Jannelle, you have to get down to the shop right now," Anita was yelling into the phone.

"What's going on?"

"Just get down here! Please!" her friend begged.

Then the phone went dead.

THREE

Not even thinking about leaving the two animals by themselves, Jannelle grabbed her purse and ran out the door. Driving just over the speed limit, she arrived at the shop to see it surrounded by police cars and a large crowd of people standing near the top of the driveway which led to the parking lot at the back of the shop. Officers Sills and Payne were standing in the middle of the driveway keeping people up front and away from the rear of the building.

She double-parked next to one of the cruisers and ran to the first policeman she could find. Officer Camp turned when she tapped him on the shoulder.

"Mark, what's going on? Anita called me in a total panic," Jannelle asked.

"Anita is fine. She is inside with the chief answering some questions," he replied.

"Questions about what?"

"Aria Matson was found behind your shop. She was on the ground at the back of Devon's delivery truck, dead. He had finished delivering your order and Anita went out to the loading dock to give him the check she forgot to give him. The truck was abandoned, and Aria was on the ground."

"It happened that fast? How did she die?"

"It looks like someone whacked her on the head," Mark replied. "It was that fast and it only took one blow."

"Can I go in and see Anita?"

"I'll take you in."

Officer Camp escorted Jannelle into her shop and then returned to his post outside. Anita was sitting in the back room with Chief Stanton. She looked like she had been crying.

"Anita, are you okay?" Jannelle asked, kneeling in front of her friend.

"I am. It was just a shock to find Aria laying on the ground. She was supposed to be at our class tonight."

"Did you see anyone out back when you went to bring Devon the check?" Jannelle asked.

"I didn't even see Devon. The driver's side door was open, and the truck was empty."

"If you don't mind, Ms. Brewster, I'll ask the questions around here," the chief piped up.

"Ms. Brewster? You don't have to be so formal with me George Stanton. How many years have we known each other?"

"I am trying to investigate here. I know you fancy yourself a sleuth, but we are dealing with a real-life death here and not a story in one of your mysteries. We haven't had a murder in this town since my dad was the chief over thirty years ago and things have to be done by the book."

"Well, let's look at who got murdered. Aria was only one of at least a dozen women messing around with

Devon in this town," Anita said. "It was no secret, so I'm sure she had lots of enemies, all jealous women who wanted to possess Devon and his time."

"Really? And you know this for a fact?" the chief asked.

"If you had been in this classroom last night and seen how the women acted you wouldn't even ask if it was true," Jannelle replied.

"What do you mean, what happened in class?"

"Devon was late with our delivery and came into the shop after the class had started. The women fell all over him, and you could tell he was enjoying every minute of it. After he left, the women glared at each other and were downright nasty to each other. Only those who had an interest or were having an affair with Devon acted up," Jannelle stated.

"They were like, "Oh Devon, my garbage disposal needs fixing", or "Can you come look at my cable box?" He promised to take care of them all and maybe someone didn't like the fact he was paying attention to someone else but them," Anita added.

"I need a list of the women who were in your class last night," the chief requested. "And put a small star next to the names of those who were acting up."

"There was someone sitting in the truck with him. I could see her when I opened the door to let him in with the first load of wine," Anita said. "I don't know who she was, I'd never seen her before."

"Can you describe her for me?"

"She had red, shoulder length hair, very pretty and from what I could tell she was of slim build. It was hard to tell because she was sitting in the truck. I would estimate she was mid to late twenties," Anita replied.

"Was she still in the truck when you ran out with the check?" Jannelle asked.

"Come to think of it, she was gone when I went out to give Devon the check. The truck was empty, and both doors were open."

"Devon delivers to all the surrounding towns around Denniston. She could be anybody and live anywhere, not just in Denniston," the chief said.

"I didn't know her. I've been here many years and thought I knew just about everyone in town," Anita replied.

"You don't have a security camera out on your loading dock, do you?"

"We've never needed one. This is the first ounce of trouble we've had here since we opened. The shop itself is alarmed but not videotaped," Jannelle replied.

"The key is going to be finding the redhead who Anita saw in the truck," the chief stated. "I think it would be best if you closed the shop for the remainder of the day. We are still processing the back parking lot area and your customers won't have anywhere to park."

"That's fine. There's only two more hours anyway," Anita replied. "Will you have to get into the shop for anything?"

"No, you can lock up. Anita, if you think of anything else please give me a call," the chief said, heading to the back door.

"I will and I apologize for being so hysterical when you first got here. I've never seen a dead body before, except one lying in a casket that is."

"There's nothing to apologize for. It was a gruesome scene, and I probably would have flipped out too, if I had come upon it unexpectedly. I'll be in touch."

Jannelle locked the front door and stuck a handwritten sign in the window explaining why they were closed and that they would reopen the following morning. She returned to the back room where she found her friend struggling to open a bottle of wine.

"My nerves are shot. Can you open this for me?"

"Going to try the new apple wine, huh?" Jannelle asked, popping the cork and pouring a glass of wine for her friend. "Are you going to be okay to drive home? Do you want me to call Sid and have him pick you up?"

"Truthfully, I'm surprised he hasn't heard about this yet and showed up here to check on us," Anita replied, sipping the wine after smelling it. "This wine is excellent. Have some with me."

"Oh, this is good. Just a faint hint of cinnamon and lots of apple taste. It's sweet and I love sweet wines," her friend replied, filling her glass a little more.

"I wonder if the chief will call Aria's mom and dad. They moved to Maine a while ago and someone should let them know what happened to their daughter," Anita stated.

"I'm sure George will call them," Jannelle replied. "He's good like that."

"You've known the chief for a long time, haven't you?" Anita asked, pouring herself some more wine.

"Since kindergarten. I've known his wife, Millie, since middle school. George has always been a very dear friend. He helped me through my divorce and has always been there when I needed him to be over the years."

"He and Sid are on the same bowling team. Sid really likes the chief and would trust him with his life if need be," Anita said. "I think most of the town feels that way about him."

"He is very well liked and extremely smart. This is going to test his abilities as police chief, I'm afraid, as I don't ever remember anything like this happening in this town in recent years. I was really young when Mr. Roberts killed his wife back in the day when George's father was the chief."

"I wasn't even living here back then," Anita replied. "But Sid talks about it every now and then. His dad was Mr. Robert's partner in a construction company over in Yarmouth and the company fell apart after the murder. That's when his dad went into the postal service and Sid followed in his footsteps."

"Sid is well liked around here, too," Jannelle stated. "For most people, he's the only mailman they have ever known, at least in this part of town."

"Yea, not many people can say they have had the same job let alone the same route for over thirty years. I'm very proud of my husband," Anita replied. "When he does retire it will be well deserved."

"Class ought to be really interesting on Saturday. Most of the people coming to make wreaths were here for the painting class last night. We'll have to listen to the conversations during the class to see if anyone knows anything about what happened to Aria," Jannelle said, getting up to throw her disposable wine glass in the trash. "I'm going to head home. I left in such a hurry Picasso and Petunia were left with each other in the same room. I hope the cat didn't beat up the dog while I was gone."

"Not Picasso, he wouldn't do that."

"He hasn't done anything like that up to this point. Let's just hope he keeps his record intact. Are you good to lock up?"

"Yea, I will be right out the door behind you," Anita said. "See you tomorrow."

Jannelle drove home running names and ideas through her head trying to figure out who could have murdered the young hairdresser. There were a huge number of suspects, and not just in Denniston. The list of women who Devon was seeing and who maybe could be so jealous they would murder someone to keep the delivery man to themselves, was going to make a massive amount of work for the chief.

On top of that, Devon had disappeared. Maybe he killed Aria when they got into a fight about him seeing other women. And who was the red head sitting in the truck? There were so many questions which needed to be answered.

She knew Devon had been seeing quite a few women at the same time, but Jannelle didn't know married women were included in the mix, at least not until she heard the conversations the previous night. It was quite an eye opener to see the spell the delivery man held over all of them and how possessive they were of him.

Jealousy and greed were the top two reasons for murder, and it was obvious to Jannelle the reason had to be jealousy. Devon had no money to speak of and he lived in a small two-room cottage on the end of town.

It has to be someone who wanted Devon all to herself. Or was Devon the killer because he wanted to stay single and not be tied down like Aria might have been demanding?

Jannelle pulled into her driveway and saw Picasso sleeping in the window.

I hope Petunia is okay.

She opened the door and Petunia was there to greet her, tail wagging. The dog looked no worse than she had when Jannelle left the house. She snapped on her leash and took her out. The dog quickly did her business and strained to return to the house. They no sooner returned to the mudroom and Jannelle turned to close the door when she saw a coyote wander through the back yard sniffing the spots where Petunia had just relieved herself.

"What a smart dog," she said, bending down and patting the dog. "You knew that old coyote was out there, didn't you? You deserve a treat."

She threw a chicken Alfredo microwave dinner in the microwave and went to get comfortable in her pajamas and robe. When she returned from upstairs, the cat jumped down from the window looking for his supper of wet food.

"You are such a good cat. I know deep down you just don't care and it's easier to ignore any other animal I bring into the house, but you could be a stinker and you're not," she said, setting down Picasso's plate of food. "Come on, Petunia. Your dish is over here."

The two animals ate in their separate corners while Jannelle ate her supper at the table keeping an eye on both of them. Petunia finished her food first but never went near the cat while he ate. Instead, the dog went into the living room and settled into her new dog bed and closed her eyes.

Picasso cleaned his dish and left the kitchen. Jannelle figured he would jump up into the bay window, clean himself and go to sleep. She was quite shocked when she walked into the living room and saw the cat and dog sleeping side by side in the dog bed. It brought tears to her eyes as she hoped Mrs. Sanderson was watching from above and knew her baby had found her forever home.

She pulled out the new mystery she had checked out from the library the day before and sat in her recliner with a glass of the apple wine she had brought home with her from the shop. She had only got a few pages in when she heard a whining coming from the side of the chair. Petunia wanted to sit with her while she read.

Jannelle picked up the dog and she settled in between her legs on the raised foot section of the recliner. Seconds later, Picasso, not wanting to be left out, jumped up and settled on the over-stuffed arm of the chair.

"Good thing I don't take up much of the chair," Jannelle said, laughing at her two roommates, returning to her reading.

At ten o'clock she closed the book and shooed the animals off the chair. She made sure the doors were locked and picked up Petunia to take her upstairs. Picasso always came up later after his owner had settled into bed and the lights were out.

The doors off the upstairs hallway were all closed to keep the dog out and a small gate had been placed in the bedroom doorway to keep the dog from wandering during the night. Picasso could very easily jump over the gate and go to and from the bedroom when he wanted.

Jannelle went to brush her teeth and when she came out the dog was already asleep in her bed. She shut out the lights and a loud sigh came from the direction of the dog bed. A short time later, Picasso jumped up on the bed and settled in on the pillow next to her owner's pillow. The family was ready for bed.

The screened in porch was like a speedway the next morning. The dog would chase the cat and in the next moment the cat would be chasing the dog. Things settled down when breakfast was served. Jannelle decided to take them both to the shop as it would be a long day because of the craft class in the evening, which meant she wouldn't get home until after nine.

She strapped the two crates into the back seat and went to work. Anita was already there with her husband having a cup of coffee in the back room. Jannelle towed in the crates, set up the gate between the classroom and the back room and let the animals out to roam. Petunia went right to Sid recognizing the postman who had been to the Sanderson house many times.

"Hello, Petunia," he said, patting the dog. "She is a good dog. Mrs. Sanderson trained her well. Watch this."

He waved his finger in a circle and the dachshund ran in a circle. He put a fist in the air and the dog laid down.

"How do you know so much about Petunia's tricks?" Jannelle asked.

"I used to bring her treats when I delivered the mail, but Mrs. Sanderson wouldn't let the dog have it until she performed a trick. She's really quite smart and knows lots of commands," Sid answered, pulling a treat out of his mailbag for the dog. "Good girl, Petunia."

"Before I forget, did you take the wreath home with you that was hanging on the front door?" Anita asked.

"No, I didn't. It was there yesterday when I locked the door. Is it missing?" Jannelle asked.

"It is. Maybe it just blew off in the wind last night. I'll take a walk around outside and see if I can spot it."

"I'll walk with you," Sid offered.

"You check out front along Main Street and I'll look around the parking lot out back," Jannelle said.

They agreed to meet back inside in twenty minutes. Jannelle started in the alley between the shop and the store next door. Seeing nothing she moved to the area near the loading dock. As she poked around pushing aside leaves with her foot, something shiny caught her eye. It was an earring, a gold hoop earring, and it was right in the area of where Devon's truck had been parked the previous day before the police had it towed away.

Darn, I shouldn't have picked this up with my bare hand. Now my prints will be on it. I wonder if the killer lost this earring in the scuffle.

She tucked the earring in her pocket and made a mental note to call the chief when she returned inside. After walking the perimeter of the parking lot and not finding the wreath, she returned inside to join Anita and Sid. They hadn't found it either.

"I guess I made it too pretty and someone walked off with it," Jannelle said. "What is happening in this town?"

"I don't know but I don't like it. First Aria and now this. What's next?" Sid asked, refilling his coffee cup. "Oh, and Devon's still missing."

"Did you know about all Devon's side relationships?" Jannelle asked.

"Let's just say I have seen him come out of more than one residence in my travels along my mail route," Sid replied. "In several cases I caught him sneaking out the back door trying not to be seen."

"They must have been the homes of the married women he was seeing," Anita said.

"It was."

"Look what I found out near where the delivery truck had been parked," Jannelle said, holding up the gold earring. "Maybe it belongs to the killer."

"You need to turn it over to the chief," Sid stated.

"I'll call him right now, and then I need to take Petunia out before I set up the classroom for tonight's project. Do we have a total number of students?"

"Twenty-one, well, twenty now with Aria gone. The wreath on the door brought people in off the street to sign up. The others are repeat students from the painting class."

"We'll have to keep our ears open tonight and see if we can help out by picking up any leads. This group loves to gossip and outright brag on things. It should be easy to get them involved in conversations about Devon or Aria," Jannelle replied. "Excuse me while I call the chief."

Petunia found her bed under the table and curled up in a ball and went to sleep. Picasso hopped up in the front display window and fell asleep in the warmth of the sunbeams coming in the window. The two women went to work setting up the classroom for the craft class that night.

"Did you call the chief?" Anita asked, placing spools of thin wire on the table between every two seats.

"I did. He said he would be over when he finished his shift to pick up the earring."

"You know, it could have been out there for quite a while and have nothing to do with the murder," Anita stated.

"That's true, but that will be for the chief to determine," Jannelle replied. "I'm still trying to figure out who the red head was in the front seat of the truck."

"I'd never seen her before, but then again, I never left the house much before we opened the shop. It's too bad you weren't here at the time and saw her. You might have known who she was."

The tables were full of items to complete the wreaths. Spools of ribbon were hung on the side wall on dowels in six rows, giving the students a nice choice of colors and patterns to make their bows with.

"I guess I have time to make another sample wreath, seeing as the other one disappeared. I'm going to take Petunia out first. She's about due."

"She's sleeping so soundly. Let's let her sleep until she wakes up on her own or until right before the students start to arrive. I'm sure everyone will be happy she found a good home and will want to talk to her and pet her," Anita said. "Most of them probably know Petunia from her walks with Mrs. Sanderson through town."

Two wreaths were completed, one by each woman, and hung up at the front of the room for sample wreaths for the students to look at while creating their own. Jannelle's was more Christmassy, as she used holly, red berries and her favorite tartan ribbon. Anita's wreath was done in a pastel and silver-glittery variety of flowers and sprayed with fake snow. Two totally different styles showcasing the difference of the two owners of the Paint and Sip.

Petunia had woken up and was whining at the gate.

"I guess now she needs to go out," Jannelle said. "Perfect timing on her part."

She clipped on the dog's leash and took her out the back door and down the loading dock ramp. They walked around in the parking lot for several minutes when Petunia stopped and started to growl. She was staring at a clump of bushes next to Jannelle's car.

"What's the matter, girl? What do you see?"

The bushes moved and the dog's growl became louder.

FOUR

"Who's there? Show yourself!" Jannelle yelled.

A figure, dressed in black, stood up. Jannelle caught a quick glimpse of the face under the hoodie.

"Devon! What are you doing scaring me like that? Get out of there!"

When he realized she knew who he was, he bolted from the bushes, knocking her off her feet on his way across the parking lot. She rolled over and watched him disappear behind the building three stores down. Petunia was barking and straining to run after him. She kept a tight hold of the leash while attempting to stand up again.

Anita heard the frantic barking of the dog and came out to see what was going on. She saw her friend and ran to her to assist her by taking the dog's leash.

"What happened?" she asked, picking up Petunia to try to calm her down.

"Devon was hiding in the bushes and Petunia saw him. He ran when I called out his name," she replied, brushing the dirt and dead leaves off her jeans.

"Why would he run? You've known him since he was a little boy."

"I have. But his face, it spooked me."

"What do you mean?"

"He was afraid, truly afraid of something."

"Afraid of what? Getting caught because he killed Aria?" Anita asked as they walked back to the shop.

"I don't know, but the first thing I need to do is call the chief and tell him Devon was here. They have been looking for him since yesterday."

"If he's coming here to pick up the earring why not just tell him then?"

"Because if I call him now, he can tell the other officers out on patrol to keep a look out for him in this area. Devon can't go home because they're probably watching his place, so he has to have somewhere else to hide," Jannelle reasoned.

Picasso had woken up from his afternoon nap and found all the new things on the tables to play with. He particularly liked the fake fruits as they were small enough for him to fit in his mouth and carry around. He got tangled up in the vines and needed Jannelle's help to get out of the mess he had gotten himself into. She set him on the floor and shooed him into the back room.

Jannelle was straightening out the items on the table as the first students started to arrive. The women went straight for the refreshment table to pick out what wine they wanted to sample for the evening. The newly delivered apple wine was on ice along with a pink blush from the local vineyard.

Half the class had arrived and were taste-testing the two different wines when the chief came through the front door. They all looked up and nodded their hellos to him.

"Hi, honey. Are you looking for me?" his wife asked.

"No, I'm here to pick up an earring that was found out near the loading dock. I didn't realize you had a class tonight. I was going home after I left here," he replied, kissing her on the cheek.

"I know, I usually only attend the painting classes, but the wreath was so pretty that was hanging on the front door here, I wanted to make one for our house. I hope you don't mind."

"I don't mind at all. I guess I'll go down the street and get a beer and burger," the chief said. "Now, Jannelle, where is that earring?"

"Excuse me. I need to get out back," Jannelle said, trying to get by the women who were patting the cat and dog at the gate.

"Here you go," she said, handing the baggie to the chief. "I did pick it up when I found it on the ground so my prints will be on it."

"Did you find Devon in town here?"

"No, I'm afraid he was long gone by the time you called me. We haven't had any luck finding the red head who was in the truck with him either. They have both gone into hiding."

"Not meaning to eavesdrop, but I have seen Devon riding around with *that* woman before. She's not from around here," Sally Andrews, the owner of the local hair salon said. "And I don't know who she is."

"Are they dating?" the chief asked.

"I should say not. I know Devon has, shall we say, a reputation for playing the field, but that field has been narrowed down and now with Aria's death I dare say a lot more women will be avoiding Devon all together."

"Does that include you?" Millie asked. "Are you still going to be sneaking around and seeing Devon behind your husband's back?"

"Not that it's any of your business but my husband and I are done. He filed for divorce two weeks ago," Sally replied, glaring at Millie.

"Is it because you were seeing Devon?" the chief asked.

"No, we drifted apart long before I started seeing Devon. It just wasn't meant to be," Sally replied. "I need more wine. Anything else you need to know; I'll be making my wreath."

"Well, at least she didn't try to hide the fact that she was seeing Devon," the chief said.

"Yeah, but was it to throw us off? Do you think she killed Aria to send a warning to anyone else seeing Devon? If she's getting divorced maybe she wants Devon all to herself," Anita whispered.

"Could be and there is no 'us'. Stay away from this investigation and let the police handle it."

"Doesn't mean we can't keep our eyes and ears open to listen for anything which might help you," Jannelle stated.

"I can see no matter what I say or how many times I say it you won't listen. Just try to stay out of harm's way. Remember, someone killed a young girl, and we don't know who or why yet."

"My bet is still on one of the husbands of Devon's flings," Anita stated.

"That makes no sense. Why kill Aria and not Devon?" Jannelle replied.

"Do you have the list of names I requested?" the chief asked.

"I do. It's in the office," Jannelle replied.

"Anita, the apple wine is gone," Sally said. "Should I grab another bottle from out back?"

"No, I'll get it. Class will be starting in five minutes so fill up your glasses and take a seat," Anita answered before going to get the wine.

"You can't sit there," Sally said nastily to Kristen, another known fling of Devon's.

"I can sit wherever I choose to sit. Bug off. You couldn't hold onto your husband, and I can tell you right now you won't hold on to Devon much longer either," Kristen said, sitting in the chair she was forbade to sit in by Sally.

"May I remind you that you still have a husband, or do you?" Sally asked, glaring at her competition.

"And you thought I was kidding about the cat fighting over Devon," Jannelle whispered to the chief.

"Are those two on your list?" he whispered back.

"They are."

"I'll be really interested in calling them to the station for an interview tomorrow," the chief said, heading toward the door. "I'll see you at home, honey."

"Wait! Where did you find my earring and what are you doing with it?" Sally yelled to the chief.

"This is your earring?" he asked, holding up the plastic bag.

"Yes, it is. I lost it last week when I jumped down off the loading dock after painting class. I have to admit I was a little tipsy and Polly offered to drive me home. We heard it hit the concrete when it fell but we couldn't find it in the dark."

"Is this true Polly?" the chief asked a young girl sitting next to Sally.

"Yes, sir. I gave Sally a ride home a week ago from this past Thursday."

"And that was the night she lost the earring?" he asked.

"It was," she replied, looking at her boss while answering.

"Don't look at Sally, look at me when you are answering my questions. Better yet, please join me in the back room for the rest of our conversation," the chief requested.

Sally watched intently as her employee was questioned out of ear shot. Everyone in the classroom could see Polly was nervous as she talked to Chief Stanton. Sally guzzled the glass of wine she was holding and went to get a refill.

"Sally seems a little nervous, wouldn't you say?" Millie asked Jannelle. "Makes you wonder if she's lying about when she lost the earring."

"I don't think Polly was seeing Devon. I believe she's dating Paul Wilson and they have been together for over three years. I think they're supposed to be getting married next summer," Anita stated. "If you're doing something wrong, why drag someone like Polly into the mess?"

"What I don't understand is how these women can all sit in the same room together?" Millie replied. "I'd be mortified if everyone in town knew I was messing around on my husband."

"Well, they're not in the least. And from the conversations it seems several of them won't have husbands for too much longer which makes the battle even more fierce for controlling Devon and his feelings," Anita stated.

"Don't they realize he is playing them? He's not going to pick one and settle down when he can play the field," Millie said.

"We won't know that for sure until we can find Devon or the redhead who was sitting in the truck when Aria was killed," Jannelle said. "Maybe Devon did make a decision, and someone didn't like the decision he made."

Polly came out of the back room and took her seat next to Sally. The chief walked to Sally, said something to her, and then tucked the bag with the earring in it into his top pocket and joined his wife, Jannelle and Anita.

"Can you verify for me Polly wasn't here this past Thursday and she was here the previous Thursday?" the chief asked. "She's extremely nervous about something but wouldn't change her story."

"I'll be right back," Anita said, heading for the office.

"Let's take our seats and begin to construct the vine base for our wreaths, please," Jannelle said.

"I'll see you at home with a new wreath for our door," Millie said to her husband, taking her seat.

"She's right," Anita said, returning with a file folder. "It was the week before that she was here and so was Sally."

"Finding the earring was a bust," Jannelle stated. "I guess I should stick to teaching art and craft classes."

"It was a nice try and I'm going to keep the earring just in case it does turn out to be evidence in the case," the sheriff said. "Do me a favor. Don't let my wife make a winter wreath with orange and pink flowers. Every time she decorates the house for a holiday I feel like I'm in the tropics."

"Far be it from me to stifle a student's creative juices from flowing," Jannelle replied, smiling. "But I will try to keep those colors away from where she's sitting, just for you."

"Have a great class everyone," the chief said, waving and heading out the front door.

The room was quiet for a Saturday night class. Usually, people were talking and joking with each other but tonight was different, and both Jannelle and Anita noticed it immediately. The women involved with Devon were glaring at each other and Jannelle had had enough.

"Okay! This is going to stop right now," she announced from the front of the room. "People come here to enjoy themselves trying different types of wine and finishing a craft or painting they can take home and be proud of when they're done. All you women who are involved with Devon, drop the attitudes when you come in here for class or don't bother coming at all. You are making it tense and not enjoyable for the others who are here and aren't involved in your little cat fight. Am I understood?"

Some of those who Jannelle was addressing mumbled yes and a couple shook their heads in agreement. Sally glared at Jannelle as did Kristen.

"I will not be told what to do," Sally replied, turning her back to them.

"I'll stay if she's leaves," Kristen stated. "Personally, I think she had something to do with Aria's death. They were both seeing Devon and Aria was her employee. Maybe she threatened to fire her if she continued to see Devon and they got in a fight. Just saying..."

"While we are on the subject, does anyone know who the redhead could be who was in the truck with Devon at the time?" Anita asked.

A chorus of no's circled the room.

"You could ask Brandon, Devon's brother. He might know," Polly suggested. "He just walked by the shop."

"Thanks," Jannelle said, running out the front door without a coat.

Looking up and down Main Street to see if she could spot Brandon, she saw him enter the café located three doors down from the Paint and Sip. She didn't want to bother him while he was eating, but she had to get answers and he might be able to provide them. Brandon was seated at the counter.

"Hello," she said, sitting on the empty stool next to him. "Brandon, right? Devon's brother?"

"That's right, and you are Jannelle. What can I do for you?"

"As you know your brother has disappeared since the night of the Aria's death along with the woman who was sitting in the truck at the time."

"I know, the chief has already questioned me, and I'll tell you the same thing I told him. I don't know where Devon is hiding," he stated, picking up the menu.

"Actually, I was more interested in if you knew who the red head was in the truck with him," Jannelle said.

"I don't know who she is. The chief already asked me that. too. My brother is seeing so many women it makes me dizzy just thinking about it. I told him no good would come of it, but would he listen? No!"

"How many women was he seeing?"

"If you want a specific number, I can't help you. He had at least one woman in each town he delivered to if not more, and some of them were married women. He was in and out of places he had no business being in and truthfully, I'm really surprised Devon wasn't the one killed and not Aria. Who would want to hurt her?"

"I know, it doesn't make much sense. I'll let you get back to your supper. Thank you for talking with me," Jannelle said, standing up.

"Any time. I sure hope they catch who killed Aria. She was getting ready to move away in a few weeks and now she will never have the chance."

"Where was she moving to?"

"She was moving to Yarmouth."

"Interesting. That's only one town away."

"Aria had saved enough money and bought a small house for her and her dog. The house had an extra building on the property, and she was going to use it to open her own salon. She told me it was the beginning of her new life."

"I wonder if Sally knew this. I'm sure it would take away some of her business," Jannelle said, thinking out loud.

"She knew," Brandon replied. "And she wasn't happy about it."

"Did you tell the sheriff this?"

"Nah, he didn't ask. Everyone is set on the fact this has something to do with my brother and his flings."

"Thanks, again."

Jannelle hurried back to the shop feeling bad she left Anita with the whole class to deal with. Things seemed calm when she returned, and Anita signaled her to meet her in the back room.

"What's up?"

"While you were gone, Sally and Polly had quite the conversation."

"And…"

"It seems Polly was going to leave Sally's Salon and go work for Aria at her new place. Sally threatened Polly. She told her if she didn't straighten up and fly straight she wouldn't have a job at her salon either and she'd be out of work all together now that Aria was dead and there was no new salon to go to."

"I wonder if she meant Polly had to keep lying about the earring," Jannelle said. "Or, the fact Polly has something else on her."

"I don't know, but Polly didn't look happy at all with the prospect of staying with her current boss," Anita replied. "Did you know Aria was opening her own salon?"

"I just found out when I was talking to Brandon."

"It seems to be a well-kept secret, as there were a lot of shocked faces when the news broke during the argument," Anita stated.

"Interesting. Did Millie hear the conversation?"

"She did and told me she was going to tell the chief everything she had heard. I have a feeling Sally will be called in for another interview," Anita stated. "I think Petunia needs to go out. She's come to the office door a couple of times whining but I couldn't leave these women alone together without a referee."

"Thanks, I'll take her out right now and then I promise I won't leave again until the class is over."

"Good. Maybe you can talk Millie into using Christmas colors on her wreath instead of what she has in front of her. She actually went out back and took flowers out of the bins, so she had pink and orange. The chief is not going to be a happy camper when he sees the wreath come home," Anita said.

"I'll try, but Millie is set in her color aesthetics."

Kristen finished her wreath early and left without so much as a goodbye to anyone in the room.

"Good riddance," Sally muttered.

"You know, Sally, you're not the only one in town who is seeing Devon. But for some reason you think you own him and can tell everyone else what to do," Sherry Walters, the local electrician's wife said.

"We all know you're seeing Devon," Sally replied.

"At least my husband and I are already separated and have filed for divorce, unlike you who was sneaking around behind your husband's back before he told you to take a hike," Sherry threw back at her. "And from the talk around town, Devon isn't the only one you're seeing."

"Just like you, Sherry, passing on town gossip," Sally said.

"Ladies, give it a rest," Jannelle demanded. "I said it before, if you can't get along and you make the others in here uncomfortable, you will be asked to leave and not be invited back."

"Sally started it. And besides, if I recall correctly, I saw you with those very earrings on just this past Tuesday at the salon. So, I guess you couldn't have lost them the week before and you lied to the chief, you and Polly."

Polly burst into tears, grabbed her coat and ran out the front door without her half-finished wreath. Anita grabbed her coat from the office and ran after her.

"Way to go, Sally, making that poor kid lie for you," Sherry stated. "You know what? You can have Devon, you two are made for each other. I don't want anyone in this town putting you and me in the same category and thinking we are the same kind of person. Jannelle, I'll pick up my wreath on Tuesday. Thank you for opening my eyes as to the kind of person I don't want to be."

Sherry opened the door for Anita and Polly who had returned together, she smiled at Polly and left. The young girl stood at the wine table while Anita moved all her supplies and the wreath she had started next to Millie on another table. She sat down at her new spot avoiding any eye contact with Sally.

"I'm glad you came back to join us," Jannelle said, setting a fresh glass of cold wine down next to her. "Relax and enjoy yourself. You really are among friends here as long as you don't steal Millie's pink or orange flowers, not that you'd want to for a Christmas wreath."

"Hey, to each his own. I happen to love pink and orange even if my husband doesn't," Millie said, laughing. "I guess just this once I could make him a wreath with the colors he likes and are more Christmassy. Is that even a word, Christmassy?"

"I believe it is," Anita replied. "If not, it is now."

Sally could tell she wasn't wanted in the class anymore. She haphazardly finished her wreath and left. It was like a dark cloud had been lifted from the classroom with her departure.

"I hope she doesn't tell anyone she made that terrible wreath here," Jannelle whispered to Anita. "I'll be so embarrassed if she hangs it on the salon door here in town."

Laughter and joking around returned for the remainder of the class. The women left with some beautiful wreaths and with the promise to return for other classes at the Paint and Sip. The two women took the time to clean up the shop as it would be closed for the next two days. The wine was returned to the fridge and the leftover food went home with Anita. Picasso and Petunia were patiently waiting in their crates to go home.

"I'll see you Tuesday morning," Anita said as Jannelle locked the door.

"Have a good two days off," her friend replied, setting the two crates in the back seat of her car.

Sunday was a lazy day for Jannelle and her roommates. She never got out of her pajamas and spent the entire day in front of a roaring fire reading. The dog and cat enjoyed their day at home by sleeping in their beds in front of the fireplace screen. They only time she left the house was when Jannelle threw on her fuzzy bathrobe to take Petunia out. They enjoyed a nice supper together and went to bed early.

Monday morning Jannelle sat at the kitchen table drinking her coffee and working on a wine order for the shop. Until Devon was found and returned to work, she wasn't sure of when and how many wine deliveries they would get between now and the holiday season. She was going to triple the order, so they had enough back stock to make it through the new year.

The only problem was she had left the inventory clip board at the back door and didn't have it to refer to when filling out the new order sheet. It meant she had to make a trip to the shop.

"You two stay here. I won't be gone long," she said, rinsing her coffee cup and setting it in the dish drainer. "When I get back, we'll go for a nice long walk, Petunia."

Jannelle pulled up to the loading dock and parked. She unlocked the door and shut off the alarm. The clipboard was right where she left it at the back door. The apple crisp Anita had brought her was still in the fridge and she decided to take it home for dessert that night.

Jannelle moved the wine bottles around but couldn't find the container of apple crisp or the whipped topping. She didn't remember Anita leaving with it, so it had to be in there somewhere.

That is so strange.

After moving everything around and double checking she was not overlooking it somehow, she had to assume Anita must have eaten it after all. She closed the fridge and turned to leave when she heard a noise come from the direction of the cellar stairs.

FIVE

Jannelle grabbed the bat which stood next to the back door and headed for the stairs.

"Who's down there? Show yourself! I have a bat and will use it," she yelled into the darkness of the cellar.

Silence.

She flipped on the cellar light.

"Come to the bottom of the stairs where I can see you," Jannelle commanded. "I'm calling the police."

"Please don't do that," a female voice replied. "I'm coming out."

A woman, probably in her early thirties, stepped out of the shadows. Her clothes were dirty, and her red hair tussled beyond description. She looked up at the shop owner with tears in her eyes.

"You were in the truck with Devon when Aria was killed, weren't you?"

"I was. My name is Cindy Sample. I am Devon's cousin from Ohio."

"His cousin?"

"Yes, I came out here to attend a family wedding, which I missed because I've been in hiding since that day."

"Did you see who killed Aria?"

"No, the door of the truck blocked my view, but I heard the voices."

"Voices, as in plural?"

"Yes, there were two of them, one man and one woman. The man's voice sounded familiar, but I can't place it. They were arguing with Devon."

"Come up here and get warm. It has to be cold and damp down there," Jannelle said, leaning the bat against the wall so Cindy wouldn't feel threatened.

"How did you get in here?" Jannelle asked when they were seated at the table having coffee.

"Devon has the keys for making deliveries and he has your alarm code. He knew you wouldn't be here for two days, so he let me in and told me to stay in the cellar out of the view of the windows. He was going to come back and get me tonight."

"Why are you both hiding?"

"I think Devon knows the people who killed Aria and I believe they were after him and not her. He's terrified. I get the feeling I might know who they are if I saw them and that's why he told me to run."

"Do you know many people in the town?"

"I used to live here up until four years ago. I moved to Ohio for a job promotion. Devon and I have always kept in touch. I know the people around here think he's a sleazeball but he's really a good man. He took care of me when my parents died."

"Sample. I remember now. Your parents were killed in a boating accident out on the lake."

"They were and so I could stay here and finish high school, my cousin gave me a room in his house, fed me and bought me my first car. He has always been there for me, no matter what has happened in my life."

"That's a side of Devon I don't think anyone knows about," Jannelle said. "Before I forget, did you take some apple crisp out of the fridge and eat it?"

"I was so hungry. I'm sorry I took your food. I hadn't eaten in almost two days."

"That's fine. It's just nice to know I'm not losing my mind thinking I ate it already," she said, smiling. "Where is Devon hiding?"

"I don't know. He hasn't been able to go home because he knows they are watching his house."

"Who's they?'

"The police and the ones who killed Aria. I don't know who he's more afraid of," Cindy replied. "He can't go anywhere in public during the day because he's afraid he'll be spotted. Someone did see him the other day and called the police."

"That would have been me. I'm sorry. I didn't know the circumstances then," Jannelle replied. "If Devon didn't kill Aria, why won't he turn himself in? The police could protect him."

"I don't think he knows how many connections this person has around town, so he doesn't trust anybody. I believe he saw something or knows something he shouldn't and now they are after him to keep him quiet."

"So, this whole mess has nothing to do with his various flings with women around town?"

"No, nothing at all."

"You know I have to call the police, don't you? The chief is a friend of mine and a fair man. If you agree to stay put I will have him come here and then we can hide you at my house. It's out in the country and I don't think anyone would look for you there. You're not allergic to cats or dogs are you, because I have both?"

"I love animals but before you offer any more help, I have a confession to make."

"You're not going to tell me you killed Aria?"

"Oh, no, nothing like that. Devon always told me if I ever needed help to come to you or Anita. He trusts you both immensely. A few nights ago, I thought there was a light on, and someone was in the shop. I leaned on the front door to look in and your beautiful wreath snapped and fell on the ground. I didn't want to be seen hanging around, so I took it with me instead of leaving it on the ground. I was going to try to fix it and return it."

"We wondered where the wreath went," Jannelle said.

"The vines were brittle, and they cracked under my weight. I fixed it while I was hiding here and it's down cellar."

"It's only a wreath, don't give it another thought. Now, will you stay put while I call Chief Stanton?"

"I will if you think that's what's best. May I have another cup of coffee? I am chilled to the bone from sleeping on the cement floor down cellar," Cindy said, cracking a faint smile.

"What time is Devon supposed to be returning here?"

"He didn't give me a specific time. He just said sometime after dark," Cindy replied.

"If someone is after Devon his best bet would be to work with the police. I think the chief will want to be here sitting in the dark when your cousin returns for you tonight."

"I don't know, Devon feels there is someone in the department who is a dirty cop and that's why he's staying hidden."

"Really? If that's the case then the chief should be told immediately," Jannelle said, pulling out her cell phone.

"What if it is the chief?" Cindy asked.

"I have known George Stanton since kindergarten. I knew his dad when he was the sheriff and his children as they grew up in this town. There is no way he is a dirty cop."

"Devon never mentioned the chief by name. I do think he knows who it is and he is afraid it will be that specific cop sent to pick him up and he will never make it to the police station alive," Cindy replied.

"This is serious. Excuse me while I make my call," Jannelle said, walking into the front classroom.

Ten minutes later, the chief arrived. Jannelle excused herself and went to the cellar to update the wine inventory count before she returned home to complete her new order. She tried to listen to what was being said upstairs, but the voices were muddled, and she couldn't make out what was being said.

Stop trying to be so sneaky and just ask if you can go upstairs.

"Is it okay if I come up?" Jannelle yelled from the cellar.

"Sure. We're almost done," the chief replied.

Jannelle set her clipboard at the back door hoping to not forget it this time. She poured herself a mug of coffee and sat down.

"Cindy tells me you have offered her sanctuary at your house."

"I have. We need to sneak her out of here, so no one knows where she is staying," Jannelle replied. "Is that okay with you?"

"I think it's a smart move. I will be the only one who knows where she is besides you. I don't want you to even tell Anita. This has to be kept totally secret for it to work and for Cindy to be safe."

"Will you tell Devon if you find him?" Cindy asked.

"No, no one, not even Devon," the chief replied. "And no one at the station after what Cindy has told me about a dirty cop. That bothers me more than anything since I thought I knew and could trust my guys, and now I find out I can't."

"It's a depressing thought that our town is not the quiet, quaint town we think it is," Jannelle said. "I guess everything changes over time and in this instance not for the better."

"I guess all that's left to do is to be here when Devon shows up tonight to get Cindy. It sounds like he has more information as to what is going on and was a witness to who killed Aria."

"How do you want to do this?" Jannelle asked.

"I'm going to drive up the street and return ten minutes later with my lights and siren on. I'll pull down to the parking lot behind the shop and pretend I'm looking around for something. While people are watching me, I need you to sneak Cindy out the front door and get her away from here."

"I'll pull my car up front and grab a couple of empty boxes to load in my car to make it look legitimate as to why I pulled up front."

"Good idea. Do you have an extra hat or something else around here you could use to hide Cindy's hair? Everyone in town knows about the woman sitting in the truck with the red hair."

"I have a couple of floppy beach hats in the office and a hoodie, whichever will work better," Jannelle replied. "Do you want me to come back later to let you into the shop? Devon trusts me and it might help to have me here."

"I'm going to bring my personal vehicle, park up the street and walk to the shop. I can meet you at the front door at four and we can sit in the back room in the dark while we wait for Devon to show up."

"Sounds like a plan. Let me grab my clipboard and put it at the front door with a couple of boxes and we'll be ready to go."

"By the way, thank you for the non-pink and orange wreath on my front door. My wife said you mentioned I might like something different," he said, smiling. "Christmassy, I think was the word she used."

"You're welcome. Enjoy it because I don't think her next project will be to your liking when she returns to her favorite color scheme."

The chief left and Cindy was taken into the office and disguised in an over-sized hoodie and sunglasses. The boxes were ready at the door as well as the clipboard that Jannelle made sure she wouldn't forget a second time. The shop owner pretended to be moving things out of the display window as she watched for the chief's return. She set up the easel to make people think another one of Picasso's cat paintings would be going on sale.

His cruiser came up Main Street lit up like a Christmas tree and sirens screaming. He turned down the driveway between the Paint and Sip and the crystal shop next door. True to what he thought, everyone's attention was drawn down to the back of the shop.

Jannelle loaded the two boxes into the front seat of her car, checked up and down the street to see if anyone was watching the shop, and seeing no one, she slipped Cindy into the back seat of the car and had her lay on the floor. She locked the front door and drove off. Once she hit the edge of town and made sure no one was following her she texted the chief to tell him they were out of the shop.

The whole way home Jannelle kept her eyes on the rear-view mirror looking for anything suspicious. They reached her home with no incidents and went inside. Jannelle had been away longer than she thought she was going to be, and Petunia was whining to go out.

"Stay inside while I walk around with Petunia in the yard. There's stuff to drink in the fridge. Picasso is somewhere around here, I'm just not sure where. He may jump out at you when you least expect it. I'll make us some lunch when I get back inside."

"You need an attack cat sign on your front door," Cindy said, feeling a little more at ease now that she was hidden in the house.

"He's really a big baby and a lovebug, He just wants people to think he's tough and scary," Jannelle said, chuckling. "I'll be right back."

Cindy watched as Petunia pranced around stopping at every tree and bush in the yard. She noticed Jannelle had the patience of a saint as she escorted the dog in her systematic sniff and go around the whole perimeter of the yard. They returned inside and Petunia was given a treat which she promptly took to her dog bed to eat.

"Do you think Devon's all right?" Cindy asked, sitting at the kitchen table while Jannelle prepared their lunch.

"If he has a good hiding place, then yes. You have no idea who it is he's trying to avoid?"

"No, all he told me was not to trust anyone in the town except for you and Anita. He keeps his cell phone shut off unless he's calling me to check in to make sure I'm okay."

"You said you heard voices at the back of the truck, one man's and one woman's. Are you sure it wasn't Devon you heard yelling?"

"No, it wasn't him, it was someone else. It makes me mad because I should know who it was who was speaking, and I can't figure it out. The other voice I would know in a heartbeat if I heard it again."

"You mean the woman's voice?" Jannelle asked, setting two plates on the table.

"Yes, it was squeaky. It might have been because she was yelling, but I really think I could pick it out if I heard it again."

"I'm going to be honest with you. When Devon shows at up at my shop tonight and is caught, he will probably be spending the night in jail."

"They can't do that!" Cindy said in a panic. "They'll kill him. He'll be a sitting duck in his cell. That's exactly what he was afraid would happen to him and that's why he's been in hiding."

"Is he sure there is a dirty cop on our small police force?"

"He is, because he saw something he shouldn't have. He can identify the cop but said he needed more evidence, or no one would believe him. There are other people involved in whatever is going on, too."

"I can't believe all this is going on right under our noses in this small community."

"Devon couldn't either or who was involved. It really shook him up. He did tell me Aria stepped in front of him and he should have been the one laying on the ground dead, not her."

"But he didn't tell you who it was who did it?"

"No, he told me to stay hidden because they would know me on sight and I'd probably be dead right alongside him if either of us were found," Cindy said, stifling a yawn.

"Would you like to take a nap after you're done eating? I have a spare bedroom upstairs that's yours to use as long as you stay here."

"I haven't got much sleep the last two nights. The cement floor in the shop cellar is hard and cold. I would kill for a hot shower and a warm bed."

"I'm sure my clothes aren't your style, but you can help yourself to the clothes in the closet in the spare room. I can stop on my way into town at the five and dime and pick up some new underclothes and socks for you if you write down your sizes."

"That would be wonderful. I've been in the same clothes since last Thursday. I can pay you back when this fiasco is over. When I ran, I left my purse in the truck, so I have no money to give you right now."

"We can deal with that later. For now, there is a bathrobe on the back of the closet door in the spare room that you can use when you get out of the shower. The washer and dryer is off the mud room. You can wash your clothes while I'm gone."

"I don't know how to thank you for all your help," Cindy replied, taking the last bite of her sandwich.

"Promise me you'll stay put and not run away when I leave for town. That's how you can thank me the most," Jannelle said, setting the two plates in the sink. "Keep the doors locked and stay away from the windows. I'll take Petunia out right before I leave so she will be good to stay in the house while I am gone."

"I won't go anywhere, I promise. I'm going to take a hot shower and then a nap. I'll be upstairs the whole time you are gone."

"Good. I have come up with a plan to try to identify the woman you heard, but I have to run it by the chief first. Now, I'm going to finish my wine order and call it in before I forget and miss the deadline for a Tuesday delivery. That is, if they're even going to be delivering with Devon off the job."

"I'll clean up the dishes and then leave you to your work," Cindy said. "Thank you again, and please, do everything you can to keep Devon out of jail. He probably won't be alive by morning to tell you anything."

"I'll do my best to protect him," Jannelle promised.

"I know you will."

At four o'clock the chief and Jannelle were sitting in the back room of the shop in the dark. The only light they had was from the streetlights shining through the windows. They had a fresh pot of coffee and sat in the corner by the cellar stairs so they wouldn't be seen through the windows if Devon happened to look in searching for Cindy.

"Is this what a stakeout is like?" Jannelle asked.

"Nah, this is much better. You can stretch your legs, have coffee at the ready, and a bathroom handy when you need it. And it's warm in here."

"Stakeouts don't sound like much fun," Jannelle replied.

"They're not. Television makes them look like they are, but believe me, no one volunteers to go on one, especially in the winter months."

"I have an idea I'd like to run by you, if it's okay."

"We have nothing but time, so lay it on me," the chief replied.

Jannelle told the chief what she wanted to attempt to do and asked him what he thought. They threw ideas back and forth until they finally had a solid plan which just might work if carried out. As much as it pained Chief Stanton to do so, they moved on to the subject of who the dirty cop could be and why.

It was seven o'clock and Jannelle's stomach growled.

"I bought some ham and Swiss sandwiches on the way here because I wasn't sure how long we would be here. Would you like one?"

"I'm starving. I haven't eaten since this morning," her friend replied.

"Do you want a bottle of water or are you good with your coffee? I only want to open the fridge once because of the light coming on when you open the door."

"I'm coffeed out. Water would be fine."

They ate in silence. Time ticked by and before they knew it eleven o'clock arrived.

"Do you think he's coming?" Jannelle asked.

"He might be waiting until after eleven o'clock when the majority of the stores on Main Street close, so there are less people around," the chief suggested.

"Darn, I just thought of something," Jannelle said, frowning.

"What?"

"Cindy told me Devon had a cell phone and he only turned it on when he was going to call her. What if he did call her to let her know what time he would be here, and she told him not to come? She was petrified of the thought of him going to jail and falling right into the hands of the dirty cop. She told me he'd be dead by morning."

"We'll give it another hour and then call it a night," the chief said. "If she did tell him not to come she's hurt both their chances of not running anymore. Devon knows who did this and why. We really needed to talk to him."

"I can't believe I was so stupid as to not take her phone," Jannelle said, rolling her eyes.

"It's not something you could have legally done so don't worry about it."

A little after midnight, the two friends left the shop and walked up Main Street to where they had parked their cars. They had no idea that hiding in the shadows of the alley, Devon was watching them as they left.

The house was in darkness when Jannelle arrived home. Petunia met her at the door whining to go out.

"Come on, but this is going to be a quick trip. No wandering around the yard with the coyotes out there," she said, clipping on Petunia's leash.

The dog finished doing her thing when a rustling in the bushes nearby spooked her owner. She scooped up the dog in her arms and ran for the house. Watching out the mudroom window she saw two good-sized coyotes wander out of the bushes and across the yard.

"That's it! No more going outside for you at night," she said to Petunia. "I better invest in some pee pads to put here in the mudroom."

She grabbed a treat for both the dog and cat. Jannelle carried the dog up the stairs and the cat followed. She opened the spare room door, ever so slightly, to check on her guest. Cindy was sound asleep, so Jannelle closed the door and went to her own room.

Her roommates received their treats and Jannelle crawled into bed. Petunia made her way up her ramp and settled in next to her owner's legs. Picasso jumped up on Jannelle's stomach and laid down looking at her.

"I know, it's been a crazy the last few days, hasn't it?" she asked the cat, scratching his ears. "Tomorrow you can spend time in the shop window sunning yourself and snoozing all day. How does that sound?"

The cat inched forward and rubbed his face against her chin.

"You're such a good boy. Thank you for accepting Petunia into your house. It's like you know, don't you? I know if you could talk, you would say been there done that. There'll never be a better roommate than you, my friend," she said, fluffing the pillow for the cat.

Picasso rubbed his face against her chin one more time and then crawled onto his pillow to go to sleep. Jannelle closed her eyes and went over the details of her plan for the following night's class.

SIX

The smell of bacon filled the house. Jannelle looked at the clock next to her bed and it was six-fifteen. Then she remembered she had a house guest who must have gotten up early and was doing the cooking that filled the house with such inviting aromas.

She crawled out of bed, slipped on her robe, and went into the bathroom while Petunia watched her from the bed. Picasso was gone from the room when Jannelle came out of the bathroom and picked up Petunia to go downstairs.

"I bet Picasso smelled the bacon and deserted us," she said to Petunia as they walked down the stairs.

"Good morning," Cindy said, smiling, when Jannelle entered the kitchen. "I hope you don't mind, I cooked us some breakfast. I went to bed so early last night I couldn't stay in bed any longer and decided to surprise you."

"I see Picasso has already gotten his share of the bacon," Jannelle said, laughing as the cat picked up his prize and ran for the other room out of Petunia's reach. "Come on, Petunia. Outside we go."

The dog and cat had been fed and the two women sat at the table together to eat breakfast. Jannelle was trying to figure out a way to broach the subject of whether or not Cindy had warned Devon not to return to the shop.

"Okay, I'm just going to come out and ask it. Did you warn your cousin not to come to the shop last night when he called you to check in?" Jannelle asked, watching for Cindy's reaction to the question.

"I never heard from Devon last night. I assumed he was with you people at the police station and couldn't call me," Cindy answered. "Why? Didn't he show up to get me?"

"No, he didn't. The chief and I sat there until after midnight waiting for him. Are you sure you didn't tip him off we were there?"

"I swear, he never called me. I hope nothing has happened to him. Maybe he saw you through the windows and ran away."

"Could be. The chief really needed to talk to him to move this case forward."

"I'm sorry. No one wants this to be over more than me. I want to be able to go home without the fear of someone coming after me because they think I know something."

"Would you be willing to participate in a plan I have come up with to flush out who the woman was you heard at the back of the truck?"

"Definitely. I would know her voice anywhere. What do you need me to do?"

Jannelle explained what she had in mind for that night's activities. Cindy agreed to the plan and would be waiting to be picked up later on in the day when Jannelle would use the excuse of bringing the animals home before the start of class.

"Are you sure you feel safe enough to stay here all day by yourself? I won't be back until four o'clock to get you."

"I'm sure. I stay away from the windows and have been wearing my knit hat around the house to cover my red hair in case anyone passes by and sees me in here."

"Great, then everything's a go and I can call Chief Stanton and let him know. Now, I have to go out and fill my feeders and sit on the porch with my coffee for a bit so if anyone is watching the house it looks like I'm following my normal daily routine."

"I love to listen to the birds, but I'll stay inside, out of sight, and clean up the kitchen while you're out there," Cindy replied. "Thank you again for letting me stay here. I hope it doesn't put you in danger as well."

"Anita and I have taken quite a few self-defense classes over the last few years. I think I can hold my own if I have to, unless of course they have a gun, and then I probably wouldn't fare so well."

"Now I understand why my cousin likes you so much. You're a feisty old broad, his words, not mine," she said, smiling.

"I'm feisty as all get out, and smart, too. Just ask me, I'll tell you so," she replied, chuckling. "And not at all conceited."

Jannelle went about her normal activities finishing with putting the animals in their crates and loading them in the car to go to the shop. Anyone watching would see nothing suspicious or different in her routine.

There was still something nagging at her brain as she drove to work. Something she was skipping over and not associating it with the murder. Maybe if she stopped thinking about it so hard it would come to her out of the blue.

Jannelle arrived at the shop ahead of Anita. She let the animals out of their crates and Picasso headed straight for the front window. Petunia followed her owner around the shop and finally disappeared into the office where Jannelle found her curled up on her bed.

"I guess getting up an hour earlier than usual has exhausted you two," she said, thinking out loud while she put on a pot of coffee.

"Who are you talking to?" Anita asked, coming through the back door.

"The animals."

"Did you have a good two days off?" Anita asked, hanging up her coat and grabbing a coffee mug.

"You have no idea. We need to talk," Jannelle said, pouring two cups of coffee and sitting down. "I need your help during class tonight."

"Oh, boy, here we go. When you start a conversation with we need to talk, I know you've cooked up some kind of crazy plan in that head of yours. Lay it on me."

Jannelle laid out the evening's plan and assured Anita the chief was in on it and would be concealed in the back room while it was carried out. Anita was shocked to learn who Cindy was and that she was found in the shop and now hiding out at Jannelle's house.

"Good morning, Petunia. I was wondering when you'd come out of the office and say hello to me," Anita said, reaching down to pat the dog. "I brought you a new kind of treat. I think you're going to like it."

"Honestly, you spoil her worse than I do," Jannelle said, smiling at her friend as she reached in her purse and brought out a pig's ear for the dog to munch on.

"That ought to last her a few months," Jannelle said, watching the dog attempt to carry the large ear to her bed.

"I didn't forget Picasso. Here's a new catnip mouse for him, although I don't know if you want him tearing around here drunk or if you want to take it home for him."

"He can have it here. He's sunning in the window. Maybe if he gets revved up, he'll do a painting or two. The shelter really needs a boost in their finances."

The shop phone rang. Jannelle answered it while Anita went to find the cat.

"That was Singe Distributors. They still haven't got a replacement for Devon so the wine order I put in yesterday won't be in today."

"Do we have enough wine to get us through this week? Anita asked.

"We have enough on hand for the next two weeks. I had placed an extra-large order to get us through to the new year in case we had problems with the delivery. I hope my plan works tonight so we can get our delivery man back."

"I'm sure you're not the only one who wants things to go back to normal," Anita replied, picking up her coffee. "Have you picked out a painting for tonight's class yet?"

"I was leaning toward the red covered bridge in the snow. I know it's still October, but we do have plenty of paintings for winter classes. We did autumn foliage last painting class and I really like this painting. It's new and no one has seen it before."

"Great! Let's go down cellar and start bringing up supplies."

"I did the painting on a twelve-by-twelve canvas on purpose so we could use up some of that size we have in stock. I checked the paints, and we have plenty in the colors we need. How many do we have attending tonight?"

"After the last class and all the bad feelings in the room, we have several women not coming back tonight," Anita replied.

"Hopefully after tonight that won't be a problem from here on out," Jannelle stated. "We can't afford to lose too many students and expect to make it through the winter months trying to keep up on the bills."

The women chatted as they set up the classroom. Anita told Jannelle that Sid wanted to take a vacation in January and go visit his mother in Florida for a week. They decided to close the shop for the week they were gone, and Jannelle would take a staycation at home getting some new paintings done for the Spring classes and upcoming summer tourist season.

Sid showed up at the shop at noon with lunch for both ladies. The three of them sat in the back room together, eating and discussing what accountant they would use after the first of the year seeing as their current one was retiring and moving out of state. He also agreed to sit with the chief and Cindy in the back room in case trouble broke out at tonight's class.

Petunia sat under the table, next to Sid, who kept feeding her pieces of his roast beef sandwich. Picasso, not wanting to be left out, jumped up on the table behind them waiting for his share of lunch.

Sid left after he helped Jannelle drag the folding screen up from the cellar to place in the corner of the back room for Cindy to hide behind. The chief and Sid could float in and out as both their wives would be present at class, and it wouldn't seem out of place for them to be there.

Jannelle brought the animals home, fed them supper, and left for the shop with Cindy, who was hiding in the back seat of the car on the floor. She parked in her normal spot next to the loading dock, got out, looked around and seeing no one, ushered Cindy into the shop. Anita ran home to grab some supper promising to return by five-thirty.

Cindy stayed hidden in the back room so as not to be seen by anyone walking by the front windows of the shop. Anita returned right before the first students began to arrive.

"Are you okay?" Jannelle asked Cindy who was seated behind the screen with a book and a cup of coffee.

"I'm fine. I hope I can help tonight," she replied.

"I'll move the screen forward a little more so you can hear the voices more clearly. I'll still keep it flush against the wall so no one can see you. Get ready, the women are starting to arrive," Jannelle said, moving the screen as talked about.

Anita took two chilled bottles of wine out of the fridge and set them in the ice buckets. The choices tonight were a red fruity wine and a pink Chablis, both from Singe Vineyards, a local vineyard on the Cape.

Most of the regulars filed in and helped themselves to a glass of wine while waiting for the class to begin. Noticeably missing were Sally and Polly, who had both signed up for the class. At the last-minute Sally came barging through the door.

"It's almost time to start. Do you want to see what you'll be painting?" Jannelle asked, standing next to the easel at the front of the room. "Here is tonight's project."

"A winter picture? Really, Jannelle? Don't you have any more autumnal pictures? It's only October. Can't you at least save that one for after the first snow?" Sally said, complaining very loudly.

"I really like it," Millie replied. "You are never happy with anything, are you Sally? I swear, if you look in the dictionary under complainer, your name is the first definition that pops up."

"How dare you? Well, ladies, does anyone agree with me that it's too early to be painting winter scenes? Come on, speak up," Sally demanded.

No one uttered a word.

"I see how it's going to be," she yelled. "You've all been poisoned against me. I want my money back. I'm leaving and won't be back again."

Sally grabbed her purse from under the table and turned to make her way to the register to get her money back. She stopped short in her tracks. Standing at the door to the back room was the sheriff and Cindy.

"Cindy...where...what," Sally stuttered, staring at the young woman.

"She's the one I heard at the back of the delivery truck. I'd know that voice anywhere," Cindy said, glaring at Sally. "She's the one who helped kill Aria."

The room became dead silent, and all eyes were on Sally. Sid had gone to block the front door to prevent any escape path in case Sally decided to try to run.

"I think it's time we go to the station and have another chat," Chief Stanton said.

"I'm not going anywhere. I had nothing to do with Aria's murder," Sally replied.

"Oh, you were there. I'd swear to it in court," Cindy stated.

"You have no proof. Did you actually see me there?" Sally said. "No, you didn't."

"I have a question before you take her in, Chief," Jannelle said. "How did you know who Cindy was? She ran and no one else in town knew who the red-haired woman was sitting in the truck."

"I don't know. Someone told me I guess," she stammered.

"Who told you?" the chief asked.

"I don't remember," Sally mumbled, staring down at the floor.

"I guess if your memory is that bad, you'll be the one taking the fall for killing Aria," the chief said, walking toward her. "Let's go to the station."

"Don't you understand, they'll kill me if I say anything and please don't take me to the station. That's a certain death sentence for me. I didn't kill Aria, she was my friend, and I'm not taking the blame for something I didn't do. I was there but he said we were only going to talk to her."

"Who's he?" the chief demanded.

Sally remained silent.

"It doesn't matter if she answers you or not. I know who he is," Jannelle announced.

SEVEN

Sally started crying and asked to sit down. She looked like her legs were going to come right out from underneath her. The chief led her to the back room with Jannelle and Cindy in tow.

"Close the door, please."

"How do you know?" Sally asked.

"I caught this person in two lies. The he is Brandon Banister, Devon's brother."

"Tell me how you know it was Brandon. What lies did he tell you?" the chief requested.

"The night I followed him to the café, I asked him several questions, one of which was if he knew who the red-haired woman in the truck was and he said no."

"He told me the same thing," Chief Stanton replied.

"Cindy, you were here for a family wedding. Did Brandon know you were here?"

"He did. He also knew I was staying with Devon at his house."

"Did anyone else know you were here?"

"The only other person was my cousin's husband to be. I was going to surprise Pam by just showing up at the ceremony," Cindy replied.

"It was Brandon who told you who Cindy was, wasn't it, Sally?"

"He told me to keep an eye out for her around town. He didn't know if she'd seen him at the back of the truck," Sally said.

"It's not real strong to go to court with so what was the second lie?" the chief asked.

"It was something Cindy told me Devon said to her. He said he saw something he shouldn't have seen.

When I was talking to Brandon he said almost the identical thing. He told me Devon probably saw something he shouldn't have when he was visiting one of the houses of his lady friends. Why would he say that if he didn't know something?"

"So, it was probably Devon they meant to kill and not Aria," the chief said.

"No. It was Aria. Devon saw it happen and that's why they are after him," Sally admitted. "Aria wouldn't listen to reason and…he killed her."

"Brandon killed her?" the chief asked.

"No, Brandon was there but he didn't kill her either. He loved Aria and was going to move to Yarmouth with her."

"So, who killed Aria?" the chief demanded, his voice rising out of frustration.

"You have to promise to protect me. You have to hide me and not take me to the station," Sally pleaded. "Brandon has also gone into hiding because they threatened to kill him."

"I don't want to ask again. Who?"

"You probably won't believe me, but Peter Sills did it."

"Isn't Peter Sills one of your men?" Jannelle asked. "I think I taught him in school."

"This is a lot bigger than you'll ever believe. Many people in this town are involved, my soon to be ex included. That's why I left him," Sally said. "Kristen is leaving her husband for the same reason. We couldn't tell people why the marriages were ending, so we made up the story we were both seeing Devon on the side, so we had something in common for people to believe."

"So, your quarreling is all an act?" Jannelle asked. "You had me fooled."

"Ray Desmond is in on this, too? He's been a selectman for this town for over twenty years. Exactly what are they all involved in?"

"A fencing ring. Stolen items, mostly car parts, are brought into the town from all over the Cape and the ring repacks the items and ships them to Miami by several fishing boats they own. The harbormaster looks the other way as the boats are loaded at night and gets paid very well for doing so. I don't know much more about how things work other than that, because I chose not to know. They wanted to use my salon as a front, and I refused."

"You can't go home tonight. Half the town probably already knows you were taken in for questioning. I'm going to take you to my house and hide you there. I need a list of all those you know are involved. I'm going to have to move quick to round them up. I believe I will call a friend of mine at the FBI bureau in Boston and see how he thinks this situation should be handled," the chief stated. "This is bigger than my small police force can deal with on their own."

"Once this is over, Devon can come out of hiding," Cindy said. "And Brandon, right?"

"They both need to come in for questioning. I want you to continue to stay at Jannelle's house until I tell you otherwise," the chief said to Cindy. "Let's go, Sally. I want to get you out of here as quick as possible."

"Good luck," Jannelle said.

"Ladies, I don't think I have to remind you that anything said in this room tonight can't be repeated.

No one gets a heads-up as to what is about to happen in our small town. I'm still having trouble believing this was happening right under my nose. This never would have happened on my dad's watch," he said, sadly.

"There's nothing you could have done, Chief. The people involved were all put in place to cover for each other. Sills was at the police station to field any questions asked and conveniently lose any reports filed in regard to the ring," Sally replied. "The only reason Kristen and I are still alive is because they knew we were too afraid to say anything, and it would have drawn too much attention if we both disappeared or died at once."

"Before you leave, I have to know. Why was Aria killed?" Jannelle asked.

"They wanted to use her new salon as a front for the ring and she refused. They needed a place in Yarmouth and figured they could bully her into agreeing since her business was new, and she would need the money."

"Why was she at the truck with Devon?"

"I can answer that one. They were discussing who was going to drive to the wedding," Cindy replied. "She was going to be Brandon's plus one. Devon never told me Brandon was there or about the other guy. As a matter of fact, he didn't tell me much at all. I think he was trying to protect me."

"I was listening to a conversation between my husband and Sills. They had no idea I was in the house, and I stayed hidden until they both left. Sills showed up and pulled Aria aside for a private conversation. He said he threatened Aria and told her if she didn't comply they would ruin her business before it even had a chance to get established. He told my husband they got in a heated argument, and she said she would go to the state police. He lost his temper, took a club out from under his coat and hit her with it."

"That must be what Devon saw. Sills hitting Aria."

But if Brandon was there, too, why didn't he run?" Jannelle asked.

"Brandon had done some work on the fishing boats for them, and they figured they had enough dirt to hold over him so he would be quiet. I don't know what happened that he had to go into hiding, too." Sally said.

"Okay, we need to go before your class gets out. Jannelle, can you send my wife back here for a minute, please?"

"Millie is done and said she would be right in," Anita said, coming through the door. "Everything okay?"

"Not really," Jannelle replied.

"Class is concluding, and Sid wants to know if he can stop guarding the front door so the women can leave," Anita asked.

"Everyone can leave," the chief replied. "In case the place is being watched, I'd like for Sally to wear my wife's hat and coat and carry her purse while she walks with me to my vehicle. Please get Sally's painting so as we walk it can look like she is showing me what she did in class. Anita, do you and Sid mind giving my wife a ride home when you close up?"

"Not a problem," Sid replied.

"I have an extra coat and winter hat in the office Millie can wear home," Anita offered.

"Great! It's all set then. Jannelle, I will call you tomorrow."

Cindy and Millie hid in the back while Jannelle and Anita cleaned up the classroom. Sid kept watch out the windows overlooking the rear parking lot for any suspicious activity, but all was quiet. The lights were extinguished, and everyone strolled to their respective cars like it was just another end of the night at the Paint and Sip.

Jannelle and Cindy were eating breakfast when a knock sounded on the front door. Cindy ran for the bathroom to hide while Jannelle answered the door. She peeked out the curtains. A tired looking, bloodshot eyed chief was standing there waiting to be let in.

"You can come out of the bathroom," Jannelle yelled to Cindy as she opened the door for the chief. "You look terrible."

"Thank you. I haven't been to bed yet," he replied.

"Am I to assume you called your friend in Boston and he wanted to act immediately on the information you gave him?"

"Apparently, they have been watching this ring for quite some time. The FBI knew it was based on the Cape but didn't know exactly where. They didn't want anyone to get away, so they assembled a team immediately and hit all the houses' of the names Sally gave me at dawn. No one got away."

"What about Sills? Did you get him?"

"I had the pleasure of handcuffing him myself," the chief said, sitting down at the table before he fell down. "I would love a cup of coffee."

"How about some ham and eggs to go with that coffee?" Cindy asked.

"Sounds awesome," he replied, picking up the coffee cup set in front of him. "We arrested nine people, locals mind you, that were involved in the ring. I don't know how many others in Plymouth were arrested as that's where most of the parts were stolen from and brought here."

"Nine locals? It's no wonder Devon and Brandon went into hiding," Jannelle replied.

"Have you heard from my cousins yet?" Cindy asked, setting a full plate of food in front of the chief.

"We have. They are coming into the station at one to give their statements. Everyone arrested this morning was taken to a corrections facility in Plymouth, so they have been removed from the town."

"May I be there to see them?" Cindy asked.

"Devon's first concern was for you. He wanted to know you were okay and protected from Sills," the chief replied, between bites. "I think he would be happy to see you waiting there for him."

"I'm so glad this is over. I missed my cousin's wedding, but I think she'll understand," Cindy said.

"It's far from over. We have broken up the ring and arrested all the major players, but our work is just beginning. My friends at the bureau don't want a single person involved in this walking away from a jail sentence. He told me this morning one of his undercover agents who had infiltrated the ring went missing. He won't give up until he finds out what happened to him and who did it."

"Poor Aria. She was trying so hard to start a new life for herself and Brandon. It's not fair what happened to her," Jannelle said, frowning.

"No, it's not, but thanks to you and your crazy, long-shot of a plan to identify a voice, Aria will have some justice," the chief replied.

"And hopefully our little town will be able to recover from this and go back to what we deem as normal," Jannelle said.

"I don't know. I think my dad is rolling over in his grave right now seeing what happened in his quiet little town of Denniston that he left behind. A lot of these people he worked with and trusted, and he passed that trust on to me. I will never be the same after this."

"Like my mom used to say, you learn from it, and you move on. You may have a little less trust in people, and you may be more guarded doing your job, but that's not necessarily a bad thing. It's still the great little town it was yesterday only now the bad apples have been picked and are gone. A year from now, most of this will be forgotten and the locals will carry on as usual."

"I sure hope you're right. I love this town and its people and vow to never ever let anything like this happen again while I am in charge," Chief Stanton replied.

"And the people love you, too. Always have and always will. Now, seeing as I did such a good job catching a killer, do you think you could do something about a parking ticket I got on Main Street the other day?" Jannelle asked, laughing.

FONDUE CHEESE AND CRABMEAT DIP

BY DONNA CLANCY

I love to cook! Jannelle and I are the same age, and she loves wine as much as I do.

Included in this series will be some of my favorite recipes, some with wine and some without. I hope you give them a try and then let me know what you think.

Enjoy visiting with Jannelle and Anita in Denniston, Massachusetts and then cook up a storm and enjoy the food!

Ingredients

½ pound of fresh crabmeat or 1-7 oz. can of crabmeat

FONDUE CHEESE AND CRABMEAT DIP

1-10 oz. package of sharp cheddar cheese

1-8 oz. package of processed American cheese

¼ cup margarine or butter (your preference)

½ cup of Sauterna wine (white wine)

Cut cheese into small squares. In a saucepan over low heat, combine cheese, margarine and wine until melted, stirring constantly. When completely melted, add crab meat and heat several more minutes. Pour into a preheated fondue pot.

Serves 6 to 8 people.

Use your favorite dippers, I use lightly toasted Italian bread cut into cubes, and enjoy!

Beef Burgundy
By Thelma Currier

2 lbs. stew beef

2 tbsp. butter

1 clove of garlic

½ cup of fresh mushrooms, sliced

FONDUE CHEESE AND CRABMEAT DIP

1 tsp. gravy master

3 tbsp. flour

1 cup water or beef bouillon

1 cup red wine (your favorite)

Salt and pepper to taste

Brown the beef in butter. In a separate bowl, stir together 2 tbsp of wine, gravy master and flour. Toss smashed garlic and mushrooms in next. Slowly add the water or bouillon and the remaining wine. Stir until well combined.

Add the wine sauce to the beef in pan and simmer covered for about two hours or until the meat is tender.

Serve over egg noodles or rice.

Serves 4-6 people.

Banana Pudding Cake
By Hattie Studley

1 store bought box white cake mix

1 box instant banana pudding

FONDUE CHEESE AND CRABMEAT DIP

½ cup oil

¾ cup of water

4 eggs, add to ingredients above, 1 at a time and beat 1 minute after each egg added.

When well mixed, pour in a greased 9 by 13 pan and bake at 350 degrees for 1 hour or until toothpick comes out clean from center of cake.

Cool and serve with whipped cream and sliced bananas on top.

QUICK AND EASY HOT TUNA TREATS
BY SARAH ELLEN

Ingredients

1 - 6oz. can of tuna

1 Tbsp. chili sauce (if you like it spicy) or ketchup (if not)

¼ tsp. Worcestershire sauce

¼ tsp. onion salt

¼ cup mayonnaise

2 Tbsp. any dry white wine

Makes 18 to 20

QUICK AND EASY HOT TUNA TREATS

Break up tuna well with a fork. Blend in other ingredients. Spread on your favorite cracker or toast rounds (I love to use Triscuits). Sprinkle with paprika. Place on cookie sheet and brown under the broiler until hot and bubbly. Serve while hot.

You can also add some shredded cheese, your choice, before you put under the broiler.

LAMB CHOPS IN WINE SAUCE

Ingredients

6 lamb chops sliced into single servings

Salt and pepper

½ cup of all-purpose flour

Sauce:

¼ cup ketchup

½ cup of white wine

1 tsp. A-1 Sauce

½ cup mushrooms (optional)

Salt and pepper

LAMB CHOPS IN WINE SAUCE

Flour the lamb chops well and place in skillet with hot butter and brown well on each side. Pour sauce over browned chops, cover, and let simmer for about one hour or until meat is tender.

Serve with mashed potatoes, rice or a nice side salad.

CONTACT DONNA CLANCY

You can find me on Facebook:

https://www.facebook.com/dwaloclancy/

or on my website:

https://www.donnaclancybooks.com/

or email me directly:

dwaloclancy@yahoo.com

Printed in Great Britain
by Amazon